THE SILVER

Best Wishes to EACH.

A. Jones

The Silver Bird

Suzanne Jones

YOUCAXTON
PUBLICATIONS

ISBN 978-1-915972-55-2
Published by YouCaxton Publications 2024

YouCaxton Publications
www.youcaxton.co.uk

To Reinhard, for practical advice and for keeping me on track.

To Jasper, my first draft reader and Wyn, my first draft listener.

Thank you.

1. Sarah

The house has been silent for weeks now, and as I sit here in the fading light, only the persistent rain beating against the window breaks the lull. The fire is a welcome source of extra warmth, but even as I watch, the glowing embers are dying down. I'm too tired to get up from this old leather chair and struggle to bed, so I'll just sit here with my little silver bird. It feels solid and comforting in my hand as I stroke it gently, and it's all I have left to remind me of him. When we first met, that week in the Austrian Alps, not long after Papa's death, it seemed as if the whole world was spinning around me. It was just a few years ago, but I seem to have aged so much recently. I was young and immortal then, just turned twenty-one and ready to experience all that life had to offer. So much has happened, but whirling through my memories of love, passion and excitement there's also grief and pain, and some things I wish I could forget. I close my eyes, but I can't forget, and I'm back in Mayrhofen, where it all began ...

❧

The early June sunshine felt warm at the base of the mountain. I inhaled the fresh morning air and stood still for a moment, filled with wonder at the shimmering, undulating alpine beauty surrounding me. But my feeling of wonder was tinged with a bewildering mix of other emotions. There was sadness and grief at the loss of my dear mother five years ago to cancer, and my beloved father just six months ago from a heart attack. But there was also a new, developing, quiet confidence in my resilience, and raw excitement at the thought of what might now lie ahead. Whatever it was, it would be up to me to find it or create it for myself, and this holiday was going to be my adventure of self-discovery. The tour guide must have noticed me in my hiking gear, gazing up at the sunny peak far above me.

'Don't be fooled Sarah, it's too risky to hike up there by yourself.' I just nodded and smiled. He was right of course, but as soon as he went back into the hotel, I adjusted my backpack, took a sip from my water bottle and set off, my new hiking boots crunching on the gravel path, my heart full of anticipation. As I headed towards the signpost for the start of the main trail, I smiled at the small group of hikers who were waiting for the cable car.

That's not for me ... I need some time alone and I don't want to miss any of the sights and sounds along the way ... the hotel is in a good location for walking, and I enjoyed the dinner last night in that restaurant nearby ... the waiter was friendly ... I didn't feel strange at all dining alone ... until I noticed that attractive man at the next table who kept looking at me ... his thick blond hair was curling around his neck and needed a cut ... but he was nicely dressed ... not like a lot of the other tourists who hadn't bothered to change out of their walking clothes and muddy boots for dinner ... his face looked a bit drawn and pale for a walker ... like he'd been working too hard ... but he was handsome and his eyes were kind ... and when they held mine for a long moment ... I felt a warm surge of blood through my whole body ... he was with that woman with the glittery earrings ... I wonder if she's his wife or his girlfriend ... she was very pretty but he seemed more interested in me than in her ... I wonder who he is and if ... with some encouragement ... Sarah! I could still hear Mamma's voice after all these years, keeping me on track as usual, so I banished my idle daydreaming and focused on the track ahead.

Two hours later I had reached the alpine meadows, a riot of colour with tiny blue, red and yellow spring flowers. I stopped to admire the view, but my appreciation of the scenery was marred somewhat by the blister that was forming on my heel. After applying a plaster, I pushed on, determined to make it to the top and back before nightfall. Another hour passed and my steady ascent had left the pleasant meadows behind.

Papa, you'd be proud of me ... you were always encouraging me to aim for the stars ... well Papa, look at me now ... I'm on my way and nothing can stop me ... not even Mamma ... she loved me, but she just wanted to keep me safe ... and her idea of safe was to marry a nice boy of her choosing, start a family and keep the faith ... that stupid boy she kept inviting to dinner ... you were so obvious Mamma ... I've finally broken free from all that ... but mostly from my own fear of taking a chance and experiencing life to the full ... I'm on my own now ... totally ... oh ... maybe I should have listened to the tour guide and stuck with the group ... but this is exciting ...

It was much colder now. My breath was coming in gasps. My legs felt like lead. The bare, rocky ground was slowing me down, but I pressed on, undaunted. Fifteen minutes later I was forced to stop for a longer, much needed rest. I took the packed lunch from the outer pocket of my backpack, ate half of the cheese-and-tomato sandwich and decided to save the other half, along with the apple and the chocolate bar, for later. *I should have brought a flask of coffee ... I need a warm drink ... oh well ... water will have to do.* Gulping down most of what remained in my flask of water, I glanced up at the darkening clouds, scudding across the sky. My initial excitement was giving way to a niggling doubt in the pit of my stomach. It was starting to snow, just a few dancing flakes at first. Then the wind picked up, making me shiver. *Not to worry ... I must expect it at this altitude ... even in June ...* as I pulled my fleece out of my backpack ... *oh no ... I didn't even think to pack some waterproofs ... I should have checked the weather forecast.* The sky grew ominous, and the snow fell more heavily, drifting across the rocky ground and blotting out the sky and the path ahead of me in a white, wet blanket. I blindly forged ahead, not knowing what else to do, as the icy, driving snow stung my face. *I can't turn back now ... I've come too far ... there must be some shelter up ahead ... one of those little mountain huts I read about in the travel brochure ... please let there be one of those ... am I still on the trail ... I can't tell ... I can't see ...*

Suddenly the snow drift under my feet gave way and I felt myself falling into a crevice, twisting my ankle as I landed. Crying with pain, I lay there for several minutes in my useless, snow-sodden fleece, as the snow continued to fall. *Shit ... I must get out of here.* Struggling painfully to my feet I stretched up, grabbing the ledge at the top of the crevice, trying to pull myself up. Each time I tried, I just kept slipping back. Then the awful reality hit me. *I'll be buried alive ... lost forever ... what a fool I am ... why did I even think of doing this alone ... HELP ... well Papa ... you wouldn't be so proud of me now ... your only child has been very foolish and may be joining you and Mamma sooner than planned.* I began to shiver uncontrollably, partly with the cold, partly with the fear of being completely alone. Here I was, at the grown-up age of twenty-one, with no parents, no siblings, no true friends, no love life and maybe no future. Struggling with the straps on my backpack, I opened all the compartments to check what I had left. Most of the water was gone, so I'd have to ration the few sips that were left. The other half of the cheese-and-tomato sandwich was a bit soggy, but I ate it anyway, for energy. *I'll keep the apple and chocolate bar for later ... God knows how long I'll be stuck here until someone comes ...*

After what seemed like an eternity, I realised that the blizzard had stopped. *Maybe I'll be spared from a snow burial, but I must get out of here!* Slowly I hauled myself upright, wincing with pain, until I managed to grab the rocky ledge at the top of the crevice, which was just deep enough and slippery enough to prevent me from climbing out. Breathless from the exertion, hands scratched and bleeding from the sharp rock, I tried to pull myself up a bit more. It was no use. *There must be someone out there ... other hikers.* Frantically shouting for help and waving my hands above the ledge seemed to yield a result, because I heard something. It was a tinkling sound, quite faint at first, then getting louder, until it was very close. As I craned my neck up to try and see what it was, several dark, hulking shapes peered into the crevice. *Oh no, it's just the alpine cattle! I hope they don't fall in and crush me!* There was no sign of a cattle herder with them, and after several minutes of bovine investigation, they wandered off.

After a few more attempts to attract attention, by stretching up, waving my hands above the ledge and shouting for help, I felt my legs turn to jelly and my hands, streaked with blood, were now turning a deep, purplish-blue with cold. Slumping down, I sat with my back propped against the hard rock and shoved my hands into the damp pockets of my fleece. I remembered the apple and the chocolate bar, still there in my backpack, but my hands wouldn't move, my stomach wouldn't stop churning, and I finally gave up all hope of being found alive. I mumbled a half-forgotten prayer, thinking over my short life. My childhood memories were vivid, taking me back to those Friday nights when Mamma would light the Shabbat candles and recite the prayer, and Papa would stand close to her side, smiling down at me. The love between them and their love for me gave me comfort and reassurance that all was well with the world, like a prayer shawl that protected me right into my teens. Then Mamma died.

Mamma, why did you leave me just when I needed you most ... just sixteen ... too young to run the household on my own ... ok ... so the maid did most of the cooking and cleaning ... but I hated her ... I had to keep checking up on her ... she was always flirting with Papa ... and on Friday evenings it was me who had to light the Shabbat candles and recite the prayer ... that was the worst thing ... the most heartbreaking of all ... I could never do it like you Mamma ... and looking after Papa ... poor Papa ... your grief was so profound I had to put mine on hold ... now you're gone too ... why did you have to go so suddenly ... I still need your love and protection ... can you hear me Papa? ... can you hear me Mamma? ... now I can finally mourn you both ... and if I never wake up again at least now I know for certain the only truth worth knowing ... that love is everything ... and nothing else matters. I whispered to the God I no longer worshipped. My face was wet with a mixture of tears and snow, as I curled up in a shivering ball. *God ... I'm so tired ... I just want to ...*

Just as I was drifting off to a safer, warmer place, I was roused by loud voices. I thought it must be a hiking group, or maybe a search party – safety in numbers! Summoning my last few ounces of strength, I started crying out for help again. The voices stopped. After a few more minutes of my cries for help, I looked up and saw two faces, human this time, staring down at me with surprised looks. One face was very familiar. It was my admirer from last night, and in that moment of weakness and utter relief, I think I knew what it must feel like to fall in love. He spoke to me calmly and gave me instructions I can no longer remember, but I did what he asked and between the two of them they pulled me out. I don't know how they did it. My ankle was so painful I couldn't stand and had to lean on him, so he picked me up and carried me to the hut, which was much closer than I had realised.

I can still remember the sight, the sound, the scent and the touch of him as he carried me through the snow. His curly blond hair was wind-blown, his eyes were greyish-blue and intense with concern for me, his voice was pleasantly low and calming, he had a manly, musky scent about him, and as his arms wrapped around me our cheeks touched. The nearness of him filled me with a mixture of joy and relief that felt like coming home. Then the physical and emotional trauma of my ordeal began to overwhelm me, as everything went black.

The next few days of that fateful week remain a blur, punctuated by isolated fragments of memory: the strong smell of soup and wood-smoke in the little wooden hut, the bright yellow jackets of the mountain rescue team, endless cups of coffee, the busy clinic in Mayrhofen (no fracture at least, just a bad sprain), boring hours spent lounging on the hotel sofa with my foot raised on a cushion, and daily visits from Hans, my rescuer, to check if I needed anything.

The first time he came, we chatted for several minutes before he went off to do some more hiking. I smiled and fiddled with the tassels on the sofa cushion.

'Was that your wife I saw you with in the restaurant, or your girlfriend maybe?'

'No, that was Ursula. Max and I had only just met her and her friend, Birgitta, in the bar that evening, so we joined them for dinner afterwards, that's all.' A slight pause and then 'I'm not married, and nobody special either. What about you?'

'Oh no. I guess I'm as free as a bird, so far anyway.' I flushed and looked away.

For the rest of that week his welcome attention was the sole focus and the highlight of each day. His smile excited me. It lit up his features and crinkled the skin around his eyes. He was older than me, by about ten years and I was helplessly drawn to him, maybe because he had rescued me or maybe because I needed a friend. During his visits we had some time to chat briefly, and with each passing day I began to wish the week would never end. One day he came with his friend, Max, my other rescuer. Max was attractive too, more athletic looking than Hans, with broad shoulders, dark hair and lightly tanned, angular features. But his smouldering look was a bit disconcerting, and his manner was quite abrupt, as he plied me with questions.

'What's your name? Where are you from? Are you English? Are you alone here?'

'I'm Sarah, and I live in London,' was all I would say in response, but then added 'I want to thank you too Max, for saving my life.' He grinned and sat down close to me on the sofa.

'Glad to be of service, any time. Let me know if you need my help again.' He placed his hand over mine, which felt warm and exciting, but I glanced up at Hans, who was frowning at Max, and I slowly drew my hand away.

'Let her rest now Max.' Hans was pacing back and forth and Max, taking the hint, jumped up, saluted to me and left.

'You mustn't take him too seriously Sarah. He's a good friend and kind-hearted, but he can be a bit overbearing sometimes. I wanted to ask you when you plan to return to London.'

'Well, my flight is leaving from Munich on Sunday.'

'Will you allow me to drive you to Munich? I can borrow Max's car for the day.'

'No really Hans, that's very sweet of you, but I couldn't possibly let you ...'

'Please let me do this for you! You haven't had much of a holiday, and you shouldn't have to walk any more than necessary, especially with your luggage.' I felt relieved and thanked him.

During the two-hour drive to Munich, we found out much more about each other. He was a careful driver, so I was happy to lean back and relax while I listened to him, stealing a glance at him every now and then, so I could commit his face to memory. I was fascinated to hear that he was a qualified silversmith with an established family business, based in Vienna. His father had been a silversmith too but had died a few years before, and Hans now lived with his ailing mother. He was an only child, like me, and he explained that his mother was quite dependent on him. They lived close to the centre of Vienna, near his silversmith shop and St. Stephen's Cathedral, where he attended Mass every Sunday, taking his mother when she was well enough. This was information I would have to process. *Should I tell him I'm Jewish? How would he react? No, it's too soon. I don't want to lose him and anyway I'm not that devout anymore.*

'Have you ever been to Vienna?' His sudden question broke into my thoughts.

'No, but I've heard it's beautiful, and the music! I'm studying to be a music teacher.'

'Really? That's wonderful! It's too bad you must go back home now, but you must come to Vienna soon. I'll show you around! Now, tell me more about yourself Sarah.' As I answered him, I chose my words carefully. I told him about losing both my parents, about being an only child, about my house in Highgate, my love of music and a little about my studies, nothing more.

We sat together in Munich airport, suddenly quiet and shy at our imminent parting. When my flight was announced he took a card from his pocket and handed it to me.

'This is my business card Sarah. I carry a few cards with me all the time. You never know when there might be a business opportunity. It has my shop's address and telephone number on it, and I've written my home number on it too.' As I took the card from him our fingers touched, quite intentionally, and his eyes met mine for a long moment. I felt that warm flush again and there was a slight catch in my throat as I thanked him again for his help. We stood up, facing each other awkwardly. I hugged him, kissing him lightly on the cheek. It was a wrench to leave him standing there, but I was silently rejoicing that he wanted me to keep in touch. As I sat in the departure lounge, I looked more closely at the card. It was very professional, with a silver border ... and in the corner was the logo of a silver bird.

2. Hans

The tourists are gathered around the pulpit, jostling for position. It's a masterpiece of late Gothic sculpture and a magnet for the crowds. I watch them from the relative safety of a side pew. Saint Stephen's Cathedral is a quiet refuge in the early morning, before the crowds arrive. Why then, did I come now? The late afternoon sun, streaming through the stained-glass windows, scatters the light into a prism of rainbow colours on the wall above my head. It reminds me again of the heavenly purpose of this cold, stone building. I kneel to pray, but as usual my mind wanders and my prayers become memories of my time with Sarah. When we met, just a few years ago, she seemed so young and impulsive. She was still trying to find her place in the world, while my own career as a silversmith was well established. I had perfected my craft, but she breathed new life into me. I remember again how we met and how it had seemed like a miracle. It still does, despite how things turned out. When my prayers finally come, they are for her. Then I sit back in the pew, watching the tourists, trying to calm my whirling thoughts. But as the memories continue to haunt me, they become almost unbearable from the news I've received today, and I know in my heart what I must do. Not wanting to return to my workshop yet, I remain seated, letting my mind return to when Sarah and I first met.

ﻉﺩ

It was early June, the beginning of a busy tourist season. I locked the door of the shop, just off the Stephansplatz, and turned to face my good friend, Max.

'How can I just take off for a holiday? You know I can't leave the shop, especially now.'

'Come on Hans, you need a break. You've been working non-stop for months and the shop will be in good hands with Joseph. We can stay in Mayrhofen, hike in the mountains, drink beer, eat lots of strudel and reminisce about the good times!' There was no refusing my old school friend, especially when I knew if I didn't take a break soon, I'd collapse.

'I suppose you're right. I'll have to speak to Joseph, and arrange some help for Mother, to make sure she's alright, so I'll need a few days.' Max slapped me on the back and grinned.

'Great! I'll book us a couple of hotel rooms.' I smiled and nodded, suspecting that Max wouldn't just be thinking of hiking once we got there.

So off we went in his car a few days later, with our backpacks and our hiking gear. We broke up the five-hour drive with a stop in Saltzburg. After a lunch of bratwurst and coffee, Max asked me if I'd like to visit Mozart's birthplace, the Geburtshaus. I told him I'd prefer to take a brisk walk by the river, to stretch my legs before resuming our journey, and he didn't argue.

The hotel in Mayrhofen was comfortable and conveniently close to one of the cable-car lifts. Max had planned it perfectly as usual, and I was happy to let him continue taking the lead.

'We can get a head-start tomorrow if we take the cable-car up to the alpine meadows and then hike up to the summit from there. But tonight, we'll have some fun!' Max punched me on the arm. I would have preferred an early night to recover from the journey, but rather than spoil the evening for Max, I decided to take a quick shower to perk myself up.

After unpacking and freshening up, we headed for the nearest bar. It was crowded and noisy, but we ordered a couple of beers and surveyed the room. Suddenly Max nudged me, indicating with a nod the other end of the bar, where there were two women, seated on stools, deep in conversation with each other.

'So, what do you think Hans?'

'They're both very attractive.' We slowly made our way towards them through the crowd, then paused for several minutes and casually looked around, trying to assess if they were unattached. They turned, noticed us, smiled and raised their glasses. This was all we needed. Max began the introductions, while Ursula and Birgitta focused their attention on us. Birgitta was a fresh-faced blonde and quite buxom, her tousled hair and tight sweater emphasising her assets. Max drew closer to her, so I smiled at Ursula and stood next to her as we stood chatting at the bar. She was, I thought, prettier than Birgitta, slimmer, but still curvy enough in all the right places. Her dark brown hair was quite short, which emphasised her pixie-like face. It was too noisy in the bar to have a proper conversation, so we just smiled and shouted a few pleasantries at each other. A few drinks later, we all went for dinner at a nearby restaurant. During the meal Max was totally focused on Birgitta. He was obviously trying to impress her with his extensive knowledge of classical music and years of experience as a violinist.

I just sat there, eating my Wiener Schnitzel, until the effect of too many beers kicked in and as I tried to speak to Ursula, all that came out was a nervous cough. She broke the ice.

'So, are you a musician too, like Max?' She sipped her wine and waited.

'No. I'm a different kind of artist ... a silversmith.'

'Really? That must be fun. Do you make jewellery? I adore jewellery!'

'Well, yes I do, but I make other things as well ... silver tableware and decorative plates, ornamental trophies, and I recently made a silver chalice and a set of ornate candlesticks for the Vatican.' There was an uncomfortable silence as Ursula fiddled with her large, glittery earrings and started gazing at Max. She picked at her food and kept sipping her wine.

'It's taken me a long time to perfect my craft Ursula, in fact, I …' but as I glanced around the room, the rest of the sentence stuck in my throat.

Sitting alone, at a table by the window, was a young woman. Something about her fascinated and excited me. She looked no more than about twenty years old, so maybe it was her air of confidence as she looked up from the menu, smiled at the waiter and ordered her dinner. Maybe it was her lovely profile and the tempting curve of her breasts as she leaned back and turned slightly to look out of the window. Her glossy black hair fell to just below her shoulders and was tied back from her face with a pale blue ribbon. That first sight of her will remain in my heart forever. She was wearing a plain top, no jewellery and very little make-up, but her large, dark eyes, ivory skin and pale pink lips needed no embellishment. She was naturally beautiful in an exotic way, which almost seemed to be out of place in Mayrhofen.

I wonder who she is and why she's dining alone in this resort, full of holidaying friends and hiking groups. As I kept looking at her, she turned her head back towards the room. I felt the thrill of her gaze and saw the trace of a smile as our eyes met. It was just for an instant, but it took my breath away. Then she turned again and said something to the waiter, as he placed her dinner in front of her. The moment was gone. *Was I just imagining it? Surely there was a connection, a silent recognition of our mutual attraction. How can I find out more about her? Will I see her again? If she's staying here on holiday, then maybe …*

'Hans, what's wrong? You look like you've seen a ghost. Are you ok?'

'Sorry Ursula. I guess I'm not very good company tonight.'

The rest of the evening was a blur. We paid for our drinks and took our companions back to their hotel. On the way, Ursula and I hardly said a word to each other. Max and Birgitta, on the other hand, were talking and laughing the whole way. I said a hasty goodnight to Ursula and escaped back to my hotel room, collapsing on the bed. Soon afterwards I fell into an exhausted, restless sleep, waking up briefly when I heard Max come back next door, much later.

I woke up late the following morning with a headache, swearing at myself for drinking too much the night before. When Max finally surfaced and joined me in the breakfast room downstairs, he looked in even worse shape than me. I was suddenly irritated with him.

'Good morning, Hans. What a night! Birgitta's insatiable and I'm totally wiped!'

'Shit! I thought we were here for the hiking, not getting drunk and trying it on with the first unattached females we meet. We only have a week and today's half gone already. Shit, I need to get some fresh air!' With that I left Max and his incoherent bragging and went outside to check the weather. The mountain scenery was stunning and it looked like a beautiful day. There were lots of hikers around and the cable-car lift was busy hauling them up the mountain. A few hardy souls were setting off directly from the base, for the long climb. As I stood there, taking in the scene and the fresh mountain air, my head started to clear. I was keen to get going. *Maybe she's up there somewhere, but wherever she is, I must find her.* I went back inside to finish my breakfast with Max and prepare for the hike. We checked the daily weather forecast.

'It looks like there might be some snow flurries later, at the higher elevations, so we'd better take some warm, waterproof clothing in our backpacks.' Max had obviously made a rapid recovery and I had to agree with his practical suggestion. The weather was pleasantly warm and sunny as we waited for the cable-car, and we were soon whisked up to the alpine meadows. We disembarked and consulted the trail map, deciding to take the main trail, heading straight for the summit. The alpine flowers spread a colourful carpet all around us as we went.

'Wow … what a view!' I was feeling relaxed at last.

After a steady climb of a couple of hours, punctuated with a few rest stops, we reached the bare, rocky terrain of the higher elevations. Max was the more experienced hiker, so I was happy to follow his lead and match his slower pace in the colder, thinner air. Soon the snow flurries that had been forecast began to sweep over the mountain. Max assured me they would soon pass. He was usually right about these things, but not this time. The snow was getting heavier, and the wind picked up, so we grabbed our fleeces, hooded waterproof jackets and gloves out of the backpacks and hurriedly put them on. Max took out the trail guide, clutching it tightly as it flapped in the wind. He showed it to me, pointing out our approximate position.

'We should keep to the main trail because there's supposed to be a hut a bit further along and we can take shelter there until the snow stops.' I was looking forward to the mountain hut, where we could get the traditional Brettlhause and hot drinks. This was a cheery thought as I was getting hungry, and I could almost taste the meats, cheeses, pickles and bread, which would be served on a wooden platter.

We trudged on through the snow, which was starting to form drifts across the trail. Max stopped and turned to me.

'We'd better slow down and tread carefully. If we veer too far off the trail, there are crevices and the drifts may be covering them up, so stay right behind me!' Max had to shout his warning because of the wind. Breathing hard now and squinting through the swirling snow, we battled on, looking for the hut.

'What's that? I can hear something, and it's not the wind.' I grabbed Max's arm and he stopped to listen. After a minute or two he grinned and kept going, shouting as he went.

'It's probably cowbells. There are herds of cattle in these mountains, hardy beasts!' But I wasn't so sure. It had sounded more like a voice, probably just other hikers. Much to our relief the snow was letting up and we spied the hut, just up ahead, right next to the trail. 'Look! There are the cattle. That's what you heard.' There was a small herd, just off the trail, bunched up together. As we headed towards the hut, I heard the sound again. It wasn't the cattle.

'Someone is calling for help. Max! For God's sake stop! Listen!'

'You're right. It's coming from over there. We'd better check but be careful!'

Just off the trail, not far from the cattle, was a large crevice that was partly covered by a snow drift. We picked our way slowly towards the edge and looked down. My heart lurched. Looking up at us was a frightened, wet, bedraggled young woman, and despite her condition, I recognised her at once as the young woman who had bewitched me last night.

'Please ... help me ...' she pleaded. Her voice was very weak. Something welled up in me and I knew there was no time to lose. I was glad my English was good, and I spoke calmly.

'Don't worry, we'll get you out of there.' I knelt, leaning over the edge of the crevice. 'Try to reach up and grab my hands. Max, hold onto me so I don't fall in.' She stretched up slowly, wincing with pain, and grabbed my hands. I noticed her hands were bleeding. 'Now brace your feet against the side of the crevice and keep holding onto my hands as I pull you up.' She was small and light and with help from Max, I carefully lifted her out. She was too weak to stand, and her ankle looked swollen. As I tried to support her weight, she collapsed like a rag doll into my arms. Max surveyed the ground around us.

'You'll have to carry her Hans. Follow behind me. There may be other crevices between here and the hut.' I gave him my backpack and picked her up. She looked at me for a moment, her eyes seeming to register some recognition from last night. As we slowly made our way towards the hut, through the snow drifts, I felt her head suddenly drop against my shoulder. *She's probably fainted, poor thing, and no wonder. She must be in shock. If we hadn't found her, she could have died.* I couldn't bear the thought.

The door of the hut was opened as soon as Max knocked. The hosts, an old couple, stood waiting to greet us, so they must have seen us from their window. The warmth and brightness of the hut, along with the tantalising smells of freshly brewed coffee and onion soup, were a welcome relief as we entered. The hut was quite small. The main room was dominated by a long wooden table, with benches placed along each side, to serve groups of skiers or hikers, depending on the time of year. There was a padded bench against one wall, so I laid her down carefully on that and removed her soaking wet fleece. Then I covered her with a blanket, which the old woman handed to me, and she started to revive. She smiled, a weak smile, but it was a huge relief for me. As I bent down to tuck the blanket around her, she mumbled in my ear.

'Thank you so much ... I don't know what I ...', then she groaned and closed her eyes again. *Thank God she's conscious, but she must be in shock and she's obviously in pain.* We needed to act quickly.

'Max, we should –' but he was already on the phone, calling the mountain rescue. They responded quickly and transported her down to the clinic in Mayrhofen. Max and I stayed briefly in the hut to wolf down a bowl of the steaming onion soup with chunks of bread and some of the Brettlhause, washed down with strong coffee. Then we paid our hosts and thanked them for their hospitality. Revived, we slowly made our way back down the main trail to the cable-car and then rode the rest of the way down into Mayrhofen. We headed straight for the clinic to check on the invalid. The doctor confirmed there was no fracture, but she had suffered a bad sprain along with several cuts and bruises, and she was still recovering from shock and exposure. Max went to get his car then we waited, it seemed like forever, in the waiting room at the clinic. When she had recovered sufficiently and the doctor discharged her, we drove her back to her hotel. I helped her up to her room and made sure she was comfortable.

'How are you feeling now?'

'Much better, thanks to you and your friend.'

'Good! I don't even know your name. I'm Hans and my friend's name is Max.'

'I'm Sarah. Look, you don't have to stay. I'll be fine now.'

'I'll drop by and see you tomorrow if that's ok.' She just nodded and smiled, sinking back against the pillow.

It was late afternoon by then and I felt too tired to do anything more taxing than relaxing with a cold beer. I didn't have to twist Max's arm, so we headed to the bar where we were last night and sat drinking beer for an hour or so. At one point, Ursula and Birgitta came in, chattering away to each other and laughing. When they noticed us sitting at a table in a corner of the room, Birgitta came over and sat with us for a few minutes. Ursula just waved and settled on a bar stool on the other side of the room.

'So, you two, how was the hiking today?' Birgitta smiled as she stole a sip of Max's beer.

'Great! How was yours?' Max obviously didn't feel like going into any details.

'Relaxing! Ursula and I slept in and then spent most of the day in the spa. Well, I could murder a strong drink, so I'd better go and join Ursula. Maybe I'll see you later, Max?' He just mumbled into his beer and shrugged his shoulders. Birgitta slowly got up and walked away.

'Hans let's take it easy tonight. I don't feel like burning the midnight oil again, so maybe we could head back to the hotel, check out the movies on TV and split a pizza?'

'That sounds great!' After paying for the beer, we waved to Ursula and Birgitta, but they just turned their backs as we left. We staggered back to our hotel, thoroughly exhausted from the day's exertions. The movies on TV weren't that great, so after finishing off a pizza we decided to get an early night. I slept well, partly from all the fresh air and exercise, but mainly because I knew Sarah was safe and not badly injured, and I'd be seeing her the next day.

I woke up early and lay in bed for a while, thinking over what had happened the day before on the mountain. Then I thought of Sarah's natural beauty and how she made me feel. The wonderful thing was that fate had intended for us to meet, after that first, fleeting glimpse and the eye contact that established our connection in the restaurant. I could hardly wait to see her, but I knew I shouldn't go too early, as she might still be asleep. I showered, shaved, dressed and wandered down to the breakfast room, helping myself to coffee, juice and a large helping of cold meat and hard-boiled eggs. The muesli and yoghurt didn't appeal. I devoured my breakfast, then went to wake Max.

'I'm off to see how Sarah's doing, so I'll meet you back here in an hour.'

'You've got it bad, buddy. I don't think I've ever seen you this taken before. She's a stunner, but just don't do anything I wouldn't do!' He chuckled, crawling back under the duvet.

When I arrived, Sarah was installed on one of the sofas in the lounge of her hotel, her swollen foot raised on a cushion, her eyes half closed. There may have been a few other guests in the lounge, but I could see only her. I stood gazing at her for a moment until she saw me. As I approached, she looked up at me, smiling, her hands fiddling with her hair. *Was that a blush?* We chatted for a while, finally discovering what we had both been wondering, that we were both unattached, there was nobody special in our lives so far and we were both, in her own words 'as free as a bird'. That was all I needed to know.

For the rest of that week, I went to see her every morning, before heading off with Max to do some hiking or sightseeing. One day Max came with me to visit Sarah. I couldn't help noticing the way he looked at her. It wasn't just friendliness. There was an intensity in his eyes and manner that I had seen in him before, when he was looking to impress a woman. He drew close to her, a little too close I thought, peppering her with questions about herself and sitting next to her on the sofa. She fidgeted with a cushion. When Max said he was at her service, any time, and touched her hand, I felt a sharp stab of jealousy and suggested we leave her to rest. After that,

Max kept his distance with Sarah, but I was on my guard with him. At the end of the week, Max agreed to lend me his car and Sarah accepted my offer to drive her to Munich airport, for her flight back to London. During the drive we took the opportunity to find out more about each other. I kept glancing at her, trying to keep my mind on driving.

'Why did you decide to come to Austria for your holiday?'

'I love hiking and I've always wanted to hike in the Alps. The scenery's so beautiful. Also, I guess I wanted to prove I could do it alone. Well, so much for that stupid idea!' She turned to me and continued, 'If it hadn't been for you, I might still be lying there.'

'Don't even think about that! You're safe now, and maybe a bit wiser too!' She nodded.

'Hans, why did you decide to become a silversmith?'

'It was decided for me. My father was a silversmith, and I was expected to carry on the family tradition. It's like that in Vienna. Many of the crafts are carried on in families.'

'But do you enjoy it?'

'Yes, I do. It's very satisfying, using my skill to create something beautiful or useful. Sarah, if you come and visit me in Vienna, I'll create a silver piece, just for you.'

'Oh, would you? I'd love that! I'd love to see your workshop too. So, I guess I must come back to Austria now!' We both laughed and it was a comfortable, happy, special feeling.

I couldn't let her just fly away, so in the airport I gave her my business card, first adding my personal phone number to it before handing it to her, touching her hand as I did so. We said a lingering, sad goodbye, but I knew in my heart I'd be seeing her again.

3. Max

The concert hall is full tonight, with an expectant, fidgeting audience, whispering to each other, checking their programmes, gazing around at this beautiful space, lined with tropical plants. The background lights in the Schönbrunn Palace Orangery are slowly changing from blue to pink to green, then back to blue, casting their soft light onto the shimmering chandeliers. I sit alone, silently watching from the last row. I can remember being up there on that stage, stroking my violin to life, playing Mozart and Strauss with my musician friends. My thoughts begin to wander, and I think back to the few years I spent with Marta. We were happy for a time, but we married too young. She began to resent my frequent absences and I felt smothered by her neediness. When she started drinking, our love turned to hate and eventually destroyed our marriage. The lights dim, the hall is dark and silent. The silver stars begin to dance, whirling around the walls. Then the spotlight seeks the stage and there they are, the music makers. The conductor strides in and the audience bursts into applause. I settle back into my seat and close my eyes. The first few bars of Mozart's Overture to *The Marriage of Figaro* fill the hall, as the music transports me to the more recent, bittersweet events that started with a hiking holiday, when I first met Sarah.

ह

Early June and the divorce papers had just been signed. I was itching to get away, but where? I remembered past holidays in the Tyrol, hiking in the mountains around Mayrhofen. *That's just what I need right now, fresh air and exercise. Maybe I can coax Hans into coming with me. It will take some persuasion to drag him away from the shop, but he needs to get away too.*

The orchestra could do without me for a week, and I was due some holidays, no problem. After some initial resistance, Hans eventually agreed that he needed a break too.

'It's all arranged, Hans. I've booked the hotel where I've stayed before. I think you'll like it.'

'Great! Thanks for doing this. I'm looking forward to it.'

As we settled back for the long drive, we had an opportunity to catch up on recent events, as we had both been consumed with work lately and had rarely had a chance to get together.

'So Max, how do you feel now, about the divorce? Any regrets?'

'None at all! Well, maybe a few, but we married too young. Thank God we never had children. We had a few good years, but as we had very little in common, eventually we just grew apart. As you know, I was away a lot, travelling with the orchestra, and she couldn't cope with that, which is probably why she started drinking. Maybe if she'd developed more of her own interests, she wouldn't have minded being on her own so much. She grew to hate me.'

'I used to envy you. Your life seemed so full and exciting, compared to mine. You were married to a lovely woman. Well, at least I thought she was. You're an excellent violinist, you've been travelling the world, while I've been stuck too long in my workshop, nose to the grindstone, working with a metal that doesn't always come out exactly as I --'

'Come on Hans, your silverwork is second to none! Look at all the business you've been getting lately, not just through your shop. You've even got contracts with the Vatican!'

'I guess I'm doing ok. I just feel like something is missing in my life. You know I've had a couple of relationships, nothing earth-shattering, and you've seen what happened there.'

'They ditched you, maybe for the same reason my marriage broke up. We're workaholics!' We settled into silence for a while, content to let the scenery flash by, each of us lost in our own thoughts. I steered the car towards Salzburg, where we stopped for a break. We needed food and eventually found a place that wasn't too busy.

'I've been here before. Try the Bratwurst. It's just as good as in Vienna, even better!' After the meal, washed down with strong coffee, we wandered around the town.

'Hans, would you like to see Mozart's birthplace, the Geburtshaus?' He wasn't interested, preferring to take a walk by the river before getting back in the car. That was fine with me, as we had a few more hours to go. So, we stretched our legs beside the swirling river and took deep breaths in the fresh air. Hans offered to drive the rest of the way, but I prefer driving to being a passenger, so I took the wheel and we set off again.

Arriving in Mayrhofen brought back memories, some good, some not so good, but I decided to put the past behind me and make the most of being newly divorced and free. The hotel hadn't changed much. It wasn't luxurious but it was clean and comfortable, as I'd remembered, and it was close to the cable-car lift. It was early evening when we arrived, so we quickly unpacked, freshened up and headed out to the nearest bar. At the time, I thought that meeting Birgitta and Ursula in the bar that first evening and then joining them for dinner, was a stroke of luck, at least for me. Hans and Ursula didn't seem to hit it off. He seemed tense and distracted. It was only later I found out the reason. I was totally focused on Birgitta at the time, and I had one goal in mind.

She was open to anything, and she made that clear from the outset, standing very close and rubbing up against me at the bar, so I could feel her ample breasts against my arm. She was wearing a very tight top, which left little to the imagination. Her blonde curls felt soft against my face and her heady perfume, although a bit overpowering, wasn't unpleasant. During dinner I kept her entertained, talking about my life as a musician. I'm not sure if she was interested, but she smiled and nodded a lot. We all had a lot to drink that evening. After dinner Hans and I walked the two women back to their hotel. When we got there Hans disappeared and Ursula, with a face like thunder, flounced inside. The women had booked separate rooms, which was convenient for what I had in mind.

We had barely closed and locked the door when Birgitta took command of the situation and pushed me onto the bed. Marta had never taken the initiative in bed, so this was new and exciting for me. I just lay there at first, watching her, as she stood in front of me and slowly undressed, pulling the top over her head, throwing it on the floor and unhooking her bra. Then, with a sly smile, she just stood there, baring her magnificent breasts. I sat up on the bed and pulled her down. After that there was a tornado of clothes being pulled off, hers and mine, and a rising tide of passion that had been building up in me for some time. I needed some time to recover, but Birgitta was still looking for more. She let me rest for a while, then she used her hands and her mouth to caress me all over. It didn't take long. We were soon rocking and rolling again. Considering how much I'd been drinking, I amazed myself, and I couldn't wait to tell Hans! It was very late when I got back and Hans was probably asleep, so the details of my sexual prowess would have to wait until morning.

We both got up late with hangovers. Hans was in a foul mood at breakfast, so when I tried to tell him about my triumph with Birgitta, he told me off about chasing women and wasting hiking time and then stalked off outside. He was probably just jealous. We checked the weather forecast and packed extra clothing to prepare for the snow flurries, predicted for later that day. The sun felt teasingly warm as we waited for the cable car, but we knew how unpredictable the weather could be at the higher elevations.

Our first day of hiking was going well and we were making good progress. The fresh air and exercise helped to clear our heads. I had recovered from the night's exertions, and I wondered why Hans had escaped.

'So, what happened last night with Ursula?'

'Nothing happened. Look Max, I like Ursula, but she isn't interested in me.'

'Maybe that's because you were distracted. You kept looking around the room.'

'If you must know, I was looking at the young woman sitting by the window. She seemed interested in me too and I'd love to find out who she is.'

'What young woman by the window?'

'Forget it! You were much too busy planning your next move with Birgitta!'

Once we'd reached the rocky terrain, the snow started, not just flurries but heavy, wet flakes that clung to our eyelashes. We quickly put on our extra clothing, then I checked the map. We needed to get to the mountain hut where we could shelter for a while, warm up with strong coffee, usually provided by the hosts, and hopefully ease our hunger with some food. I pushed on but slowed the pace, warning Hans about the crevices beneath the snow drifts and to be careful not to veer off the trail. Hans trudged on directly behind me until suddenly he yelled at me to stop. He'd heard something. I hadn't heard anything, but I was focused on looking for the hut. Stopping for a moment to listen, all I could hear was the wind. I told him about the alpine cattle wandering the mountains and he'd probably just heard the cowbells from a herd nearby. I was impatient to make it to the hut, so I kept going, with Hans following slowly behind. By then the snow had stopped, and the hut suddenly came into view, much to my relief. I spotted some cattle, just off the trail, and pointed them out to Hans. We kept going for a few more minutes, but then I heard it too. Hans was right. It was a woman's voice, calling for help.

It was the first time I ever saw Sarah and I'll never forget it. She'd fallen through one of the snow drifts into a small crevice, which was just deep enough to prevent her from climbing out. Sitting in a corner of the crevice, shivering and bleeding, she was just a wet, bedraggled heap, but when she looked up at us, pleading for help, I was struck by her large, dark eyes, which were almost too large for her delicate features. Her long black hair was soaking wet and clinging to her face. Hans told me later he had recognised her as the young woman in the restaurant, the evening before. I was about to suggest how we could get her out, when he began calmly speaking to her. Then he gave me instructions to assist him. If he wanted to take the lead, so be it. She was light and we had no problem lifting her out, but she was in pain and her ankle was swollen, so Hans carried her, following behind me as I picked our way carefully to the hut.

It was a relief to get into the warmth. The hosts, an old couple, were very helpful. While Hans and the old woman took care of Sarah, who was fading in and out of consciousness, the old man gave me the number for the mountain rescue team. I called and explained the situation and the location of the hut. They responded quickly, checking her condition and making sure she was comfortable, before transporting her down to the clinic in Mayrhofen.

Hans and I couldn't go with them, so we stayed for a while, taking advantage of the old couple's hospitality. Strong coffee, bowls of onion soup and the traditional Brettlhause revived us, and we felt we could tackle the hike back down the mountain. We paid for the welcome meal, thanked our hosts, and retraced our steps down the main trail. After about a half hour of silent trudging, Hans interrupted my thoughts.

'Max, you never got a chance to tell me what happened with Birgitta last night.'

26

'No, I guess not, but you weren't exactly open to listening this morning.' I was tempted to clam up and leave him wondering, but I had been bursting to tell him all day, so my ego took over and I gave him a blow-by-blow account, including all the titillating details.

'I don't know how you do it Max. You must have been very drunk by then.'

'Experience Hans. You need to chat them up first, get them warmed up, then the foreplay comes in.' I paused, then added, 'Of course, it helps if she's panting for it too.'

Hans smiled. 'That's what I figured. Anyone could see she was panting for it all evening.' Somehow my triumph didn't seem quite as impressive anymore, not to Hans anyway.

After more silent trudging, we reached the top of the cable car lift and were soon back down in the centre of Mayrhofen. We headed straight to the clinic to check up on the invalid. The doctor told us there was no fracture, just a bad sprain, cuts, bruises and the after-effects of exposure, but she was recovering well and would be able to leave the clinic in about a half-hour. I went to get my car and as soon as she was discharged, we drove her back to her hotel. She was hobbling on crutches, so I offered to help, but Hans insisted on taking her in himself and getting her settled. I waited in the car, drumming my fingers on the wheel, until he came out fifteen minutes later.

'She's feeling much better now. Her name is Sarah. I told her our names and I'm going to drop by tomorrow morning to see how she's doing.' What more was there to say? We got back to our room and freshened up, then decided we just wanted to grab a cold beer or two and relax that evening. We headed back to the bar where we were the night before, and while we were lounging in the corner with our drinks, Birgitta and Ursula wandered in. Hans just snickered. Ursula waved and found a bar stool far enough away to make her point, not that Hans cared. Birgitta, on the other hand, came and sat with us for a few minutes, stealing sips of my beer and asking about our day's hiking. I couldn't face telling her what had really happened. There would be the inevitable probing questions and it was none of her business anyway. She and Ursula had spent the day in the spa. They were obviously not there for the hiking. Looking at her in the bright, late afternoon light that was streaming through the window, she didn't seem quite so desirable anymore. Her face was sallow, her eyes were puffy, which the heavy makeup and thick, black mascara couldn't conceal. Her breasts just looked big, and she was too chubby. *How could I have been attracted to her last night? I must have been really sloshed!* I didn't respond to her hint about seeing her later, so she sauntered off to join Ursula. *Good riddance!* Hans and I staggered back to our hotel and checked the movies on TV. They weren't that great, but we watched a couple of them anyway, not really registering. It was just an excuse to pass the time in a boozy daze. Then we ordered a pizza and polished it off, before finally hitting the sack.

I slept in again, until Hans came pounding on the door, forcing me to get up. He'd already showered, shaved and had breakfast downstairs and was off to check up on Sarah. I groaned. *What a keener! I must admit she's a stunner but really, he does tend to get carried away!* Warning him not to do anything I wouldn't do, I chuckled and crawled back under the duvet. But I was ready when he returned an hour later, beaming.

'She's not married Max, and there's nobody special at home, so she's free as a bird! I'm going to drop in and see her every morning before we set off for the day. She's stuck there, alone in the hotel and she needs company. I know she's looking forward to my visits.'

'Well, aren't you lucky! Now let's get going. The weather's good and there's no snow forecast, so we could make it to the summit today.'

We did make it to the summit that day, so for the rest of the week we tried a couple of other, less demanding, hikes, just enjoying the fresh air and alpine scenery. One day we just took off in my car to do some sightseeing in the area, stopping when we felt like it and sampling the food in some of the region's restaurants. Neither of us mentioned Sarah, or Birgitta, or Ursula that day. We were just good pals, enjoying each other's company.

The following morning, my curiosity got the better of me and I went along with Hans to see how Sarah was doing. She took my breath away as soon as I saw her, relaxed and reclining on the sofa in the hotel lounge. What a transformation! She was a totally different creature from the pitiful woman we had rescued, but those eyes were the same eyes, and her long black hair was now pulled back and falling softly around her shoulders. She smiled when she saw us. Like a moth to the flame, I couldn't help myself. I had to find out more about her, more than Hans had been willing to divulge. I moved closer, smiling and gazing down at her.

'What's your name?' *I already knew, but I just wanted to hear her say it.* 'Where are you from? Are you English? Are you alone here?' Somehow the questions just spilled out, one after the other and she flushed, fidgeting with a cushion. *Slow down!* I had to tell myself.

'I'm Sarah, and I live in London, and I want to thank you too Max, for saving my life.' I sat down next to her on the sofa, as close as I could get, with Hans watching me like a hawk.

'Glad to be of service, any time. Let me know if you need my help again.' Then I couldn't resist touching her hand as it was so close to mine. It felt warm and soft. She hesitated for a moment before slowly pulling it away. Hans frowned at me.

'Let her rest now Max.' He was so obvious. I stood up, saluted to Sarah and left, but not before I noticed her eyes following me, registering a definite interest in me. This impression of Sarah stayed with me for the rest of that week, and it kept me wondering if I stood a chance with her. *But Hans is so smitten with her and so protective. I'd better back off. I value his friendship too much.* I didn't go to visit Sarah again and I let Hans borrow my car at the end of the week, to drive her to Munich airport.

4. Sarah

The flight back to London was uneventful, so I tried to doze off for a while, but it was no use. *So much has happened to me in just one week, more than I could ever have imagined from one brief holiday. Hiking alone up that mountain was stupid. What was I trying to prove? God, I could have died if it hadn't been for Hans and Max finding me and taking care of me. Hans is such a lovely man. He's so handsome, and he makes me feel special. This feeling I get when I see him, or even think of him, may be love after all. I wonder if he feels the same way about me. He's so handsome there may be other women in his life ... God, I wish I knew for sure. At least he wants to see me again.* I rummaged in my handbag and took out his business card, running my finger over the slightly raised logo of the silver bird, imagining him busy in his workshop in Vienna, designing and creating something just for me!

I'm not so sure what to think of Max. He's very attractive too, in a different way - dark hair, tanned, slim and athletic looking - he struck me as being quite sexy and intense, and he seemed very interested in me. He stirred something in me too. It felt a bit strange, but exciting ... pleasant and yet uncomfortable at the same time ... though I'm not sure why ... maybe my body was trying to tell me something. My thoughts returned to Hans, as I put the card back in my handbag.

As the plane started its descent into Heathrow, I was feeling smug. It felt good to get so much attention from two handsome men. *I would love to visit Vienna and see them again. I'll write to*

Hans when I get home to thank him for everything and hopefully find out when would be the best time to visit. Later this summer would be great, before my teacher-training course resumes. I think a personal note to his shop would be better than a phone call. I don't want to put him on the spot as he's so busy, and it would give him some time to consider. I hope he wasn't just being polite when he invited me. I guess there's only one way to find out … God, I'll need to buy some new clothes. Vienna is probably very sophisticated with all those concerts and palaces. I'll need to book a flight soon, and book a hotel too, near his place, and if all goes well, I'll invite him to come and visit me in London and … The plane touched down and jolted me back to earth.

The King's Cross Express from Heathrow wasn't too crowded. I made the connection easily onto the Northern Line, but my ankle was feeling sore again and all the jostling on the tube didn't help, as I had to stand. I was starting to flag. I pulled my suitcase closer to my feet and surveyed the people around me. Most of them were looking bored. I felt a rising resentment. *Why don't men give up their seats for women anymore? That poor woman is obviously very pregnant, and those young men opposite are showing no signs of budging.* I was about to say something scathing to them, but they suddenly got up and left the tube. I closed my eyes and listened for my stop.

When I emerged at Highgate Station it was drizzling. *Welcome back to lovely English weather. At least the rain feels cool and refreshing on my face after the stuffy air in the tube. It's too far to walk from here and my ankle really hurts. Oh good, there's a taxi.*

'Let me help you with your suitcase. Where to Miss?'

'Thanks! 21 Hillview Crescent please.'

'Have you been on holiday, somewhere sunny?'

'I've been on holiday in Austria, in the Alps, and it was sunny most of the time. But I got caught in a snowstorm high up in the mountains and fell into a crevice, sprained my ankle.'

'Oh no! That must have been scary. Still, you're back safe and sound now.'

'Yes, it was terrifying, but I was rescued by two really nice men.' I was bursting to tell someone, anyone, about Hans, but the taxi driver's radio crackled with instructions for his next fare. He was no longer interested in the adventures of the young woman in the back seat.

As the taxi proceeded slowly through a quiet, upmarket area of Highgate, I peered through the rain-spattered window at the houses. Large and architecturally impressive, some of them were only partially visible behind trees, stone walls or high fences. As a child growing up in this area, and even now, I wondered about the residents of these mansions, if they were happy or sad, and what secrets, if any, they were hiding. I chuckled to myself. *The preserve of the rich and famous. These are my neighbours. I must invite them for dinner, kosher of course. Who am I kidding?* The taxi kept going, away from the celebrity mansions, turning down several side streets, and finally stopping in front of my red brick, Georgian townhouse.

Home sweet home! It's not a celebrity mansion, but still impressive and it's all mine now. I paid the taxi driver and limped to the front door with my suitcase, fumbling with my keys.

'Welcome home Sarah!' Papa's booming, beloved voice greeted me from the little window, halfway up the oak staircase, then the echo faded away in a cloud of swirling dust.

'You must be tired dear. Come and sit down next to me and tell me all about it.' Soft and soothing, coaxing and cajoling as always, Mamma was waiting for me on the green velvet sofa. Dropping my suitcase, I rushed towards her, and then slumped into Papa's worn leather chair.

I sat there, listening to the silence, tasting the salty tears that had trickled down my cheeks, not wanting to get up and face the emptiness of this house, that was once full to bursting with such warm memories. Since moving in there three months ago, happy to leave the small flat I shared with Miriam, I had been busying myself with my music studies and my teacher-training course, making sure I was out as much as possible, coming home just to sleep. My inheritance windfall was dipped into regularly. It was fun to go shopping in Harrod's and order caviar at The Savoy, without a second thought. The holiday in Austria was another distraction and one that had yielded interesting results! Now the summer holidays were stretching before me and there was nothing definite in my diary, other than making some time to practice the piano and study for an instructional psychology exam, which I'd have to face upon my return to college in October.

I still sat there. Papa's old chair felt warm and comforting, surrounding me completely, like his loving, rib-crushing bear hugs. The green velvet sofa was looking faded and old fashioned now, but it was considered elegant in its day, just like Mamma. The dusty piano in the corner was patiently waiting for me to fill the empty spaces with music again. *I suppose I'll have to do something about some of the furniture ... and those old, framed photos on the wall, of my ancestors and other family members.* I had known for a long time that some of them were also holocaust victims. The faces in the photos were blurred and serious, and I had long ago stopped looking at them. I knew I could never ... must never ... forget what happened to them, but having those photos on the wall, in plain view, meant to be looked at every day, was unbearably depressing.

I'll take them out of the frames and put them in a special album, and I'll give them a place of honour on the sideboard, next to the Shabbat candles, so they'll be remembered, just in a different way ... my way ... and I'll buy some bright, cheerful prints to put up in their place. The house would need a lot of work to make it my own and I still had to come to terms with my grief and loneliness. I hesitated to call Miriam, as we had not parted on the best of terms, not really a blow-up, just a cooling off. Anyway, we were both relieved when I moved out. I recalled our last conversation.

'Sarah, I hope you'll be happy in your parents' house in Highgate, just don't be such a snob!'

'You're just jealous! You've always been jealous of me, ever since the Daniel episode.'

'I'm not jealous! I'm just not impressed with your behaviour – and another thing – I won't miss your messy habits – wet towels on the bathroom floor – dirty dishes piled in the sink ...'

Thinking back, I had to admit feeling a bit guilty about not pulling my weight in the flat, but Miriam was such a fusspot. As for the thing with Daniel, could I help it if he preferred me to her? She made such a scene about it, just because she'd been seeing him for a year before he asked me out and I accepted. *Best friend or not, all's fair in love and war.* Anyway, I didn't really like him that much. I just liked his black Jaguar, and the way we made love like wild animals in the back seat. He lived with his parents, so we couldn't go there, and we couldn't make love in the flat, not with Miriam snooping around. I knew it wouldn't last; it was just fun for a few months, then it just fizzled out. And those 'nice Jewish boys' Mamma used to invite for dinner were either painfully shy or annoyingly arrogant. *Come to think of it, my relationships haven't been that great so far and maybe it was a mistake to steal Daniel away from Miriam. It may have cost me her friendship. Meeting Hans was the best thing that's happened to me so far, so please God, let it work out!*

I hauled myself out of Papa's chair and dragged my suitcase upstairs to unpack, but I was too tired, so I decided to leave the unpacking for the morning. Instead, I chose a small 'thank you' card from the stash Mamma kept, 'just in case' and took Hans's business card out of my handbag. Using my best handwriting, I copied the address of his shop carefully onto a blue envelope and started to write on the note card. A sudden fit of the shakes ruined the first one. *I'm just tired. Let's try again ...* but my writing on the second card was too scrawly, so after a couple of cards had been tossed into the waste basket, I tried for a third time, and was finally happy with my note.

> *Dear Hans,*
>
> *Thanks again for rescuing me and for everything! I miss you already! I would love to come and visit you in Vienna, if that's ok. I know you must be busy. If you would still like me to come, please let me know the best time, as I'll be waiting to hear. Please thank Max for me too.*
>
> *Love,*
>
> *Sarah*

I added my phone number, and read the note over several times, to make sure it didn't sound too pushy, then sealed it and placed it on my dressing table, ready to be posted first thing in the morning.

As I lay in bed that night, tossing and turning, I tortured myself with the terrible thought: *What if he doesn't respond?* Eventually I drifted off into a restless, exhausted sleep. I posted the card the next day and then tried to put it out of my mind. About a week later the telephone rang and it was him! My hand shook slightly as I clutched the phone.

'Hello Sarah, it's Hans. I just received your card. How are you?'

'Oh... Hans! It's lovely to hear your voice! I'm fine ... and you?'

'Yes, I'm very well. I was pleased to hear from you. Of course, I want you to come to Vienna!'

The rest of the conversation was to discuss the practical arrangements and confirm the dates. Since July and August were the busiest months for Hans, we settled on a week in early September, before my course resumed at the teacher training college. I booked a flight and a hotel in central Vienna, which he recommended, then called him back to confirm. My empty suitcase was immediately thrown open on the bed in the spare bedroom, ready to be packed again. I liked to be prepared. There was just one problem - I had nothing suitable to wear! Well at least

I had the whole summer to go shopping and organise my outfits. I would need some new shoes too.

The next two weeks were spent in a flurry of frantic activity. It was partly an attempt to fill up the echoing space around me, but mostly it was the need to clean up six months of dust and general clutter that had accumulated since Papa died. *I'm not much of a housekeeper, but I don't regret cancelling the maid right after the funeral. I couldn't stand her. She fussed so much over Papa, as if she was a member of the family. It was sickening.* However, now I was starting to feel overwhelmed with the amount of hard work it was taking to try to get things back to the way they were, when Mamma and Papa were in control. My energy level seemed to be flagging more than usual. I was too tired to go shopping for clothes and trying things on was exhausting. That would have to wait.

Miriam hadn't called. We were friends since university, where we first met, both graduating with a B.A. in Music, both enrolling in the teacher-training course. We'd shared the flat for two years after I left home, and we had so many interests in common. *She could at least call and ask about my holiday. Then I could tell her about Hans. Maybe I should call her. It would be nice to meet for coffee ... then again maybe not. She's probably still angry with me.* Miriam had been my only friend for so long, I didn't know where to turn and I was feeling the need for some company. Then I thought of the synagogue. I hadn't been there for ages, even though Mamma and Papa had attended regularly, so I wondered how I would be received. It was Saturday morning, so I decided to wander along and attend the service. I needn't have worried.

'Shalom Sarah! How are you coping? You look tired.' Mamma's friend, Ruth, hugged me.

'I've been on holiday and now I'm trying to get the house cleaned up, but it's hard work.'

'You can't do it all alone. You must get some help. I'll ask my cleaning service to give you a call. They're very good. Are you eating properly?' It felt a bit strange to sit there again with my

Jewish neighbours for the Torah reading, but I was glad I had decided to return to the fold. Most of all I welcomed the attention. I received several invitations to Shabbat on Friday evenings, and I was happy to accept.

Through the rest of the summer, those warm, friendly gatherings helped me to slow down, relax and calm my mind. The soothing, repetitive rituals of the blessings over candles, blessing the wine and the challah, the special meal, followed by more blessings, were slightly different with each family I visited. But they reminded me of my own family's traditions.

My Shabbat usually began with the warm smell of Mamma's freshly baked challah, strangely mixed with the scent of Mamma's sandalwood perfume. She always wore it on Friday evenings. Traditionally, Friday evenings were meant to be when husbands and wives made love, so Mamma wanted to look (and smell) attractive. It always worked, because Papa would gaze at her, a boyish smile lighting up his face, and then he'd start singing with that strong voice of his, while I played the piano. Mamma pretended not to notice his admiring glances as she fussed over the special meal. As she cooked, other tantalising smells would gradually fill up the house. When the meal was ready, Mamma would carry the old pewter candlesticks to the table and light three candles. The first two traditional candles symbolised light and darkness, female and male, and the extra one was for me. Sometimes she would let me light the third candle. She recited the blessing over the candles, while making a large circle over the flames with her arms. Then she would cover her face in prayer. I used to think she was crying, but it was only the traditional blessing. The meal was always the same: home-made chicken soup, followed by slow-cooked beef, plain boiled potatoes and whatever other vegetables were in season. There was always fresh fruit and cake to follow.

Papa's favourite Shabbat song, which became our own family ritual, was "Shalom Aleichem". He sang it in Hebrew, but years ago he had translated it:

Peace be yours, angels of peace ...
Angels of the most high ...
Angel of the King who is King of kings ...
The holy blessed One.

As a child, I loved the singing ritual, and all the other rituals and blessings, which made the family Friday evening Shabbat such a special, happy occasion. However, there were times, as a teenager, when I yearned to be out with my friends on Friday evenings, and then I would plead my case with Papa. He always relented, while Mamma frowned and shook her head, but eventually she gave in to him and I escaped. It was only now that I was beginning to fully appreciate how important these rituals were, for every Jewish family, and to realise how lucky I was to belong to the Jewish community. My grief was starting to ease a little, replaced by love and gratitude.

Once the cleaning service had begun working its miracles, I felt more relaxed and able to focus my attention on other things. The summer was well underway and the small garden behind the house was a shambles. It had been left to the weeds for months and was crying out for attention. *Maybe I'll be a better gardener than housekeeper.* Pulling weeds and cutting back the overgrown bushes was just as tiring as the drudgery of housework, but it was therapeutic. I felt more connected to the earth and the natural cycles of growth, decay and rebirth.

One day I found a small rosebush hiding under a tangle of brambles, looking bedraggled and forlorn. It was the one Mamma had planted years ago and I remember how she had tended it so lovingly. It took a while to flower, but Mamma kept up the feeding and watering, coaxing and cajoling, until it finally gave in to her and bloomed with a profusion of pink roses. I cleared away all the brambles, pruned the dying stems, watered and fed it, as Mamma had done, and went out in the garden almost every day to check on progress. I rejoiced when I saw a couple of tiny green leaves beginning to sprout. It was my special project and a way to honour

Mamma. For Papa, I planted a tree. It was just a sapling, but I knew, with loving care, it would in time grow tall and sturdy, just like him. When grief crept up on me as I worked, it was somehow more bearable now and it kept me close to them.

Playing the piano helped too. Papa always said I played beautifully, so I kept practicing for him. My favourite pieces were Mozart's Piano Sonatas, maybe because they were serene and restful and as I played, I could daydream about my upcoming trip to Vienna, maybe attending concerts, but mostly seeing Hans again. *I wonder what he's doing now and if he's thinking about me and I wonder what it would feel like if we kissed and embraced ... and then ... God ... I can hardly wait!* The music filled all the empty spaces in my house, and my thoughts of Hans filled all the empty spaces in my heart. Occasionally, as I played, my hands would feel a bit stiff and tingly, and I would have to rest them for a while and start over, but I kept practising and felt I was progressing well. Studying for my instructional psychology exam wasn't quite as enjoyable. I struggled to see the relevance of the abstract theories to practical teaching methods, and after sitting still for hours I would get painful spasms in my legs. However, I kept at it, because I was determined to pass the exam.

As late summer wore on and the weather was good, I decided to invite a few guests over for tea or lunch in the garden, to thank the families who had been so kind to me. I had never been much of a cook, so I had to keep things simple. When I was at university I used to eat at cheap, fast-food places and cheeseburgers were my staple diet. This broke the kosher laws, mixing meat with milk products, but my parents never knew so it didn't bother me. Miriam did most of the cooking at the flat and I'd be stuck with the dishes. When it was my turn to cook, I ordered pizza or served beef sausages and baked beans. *There must be a way I can improve my cooking without breaking the kosher laws.* After poring over Mamma's stack of kosher recipes, which looked complicated, I came to a decision. *From now on I'm strictly vegetarian. Cutting out meat and fish won't break any kosher laws or offend anyone, and it's good for the planet.* So, I picked out a few vegetarian recipes and practiced on myself. While I enjoyed making and eating tomato, mushroom and asparagus quiche, vegetable lasagne and all kinds of weird and wonderful salads, I did get the odd craving to sink my teeth into a big, messy cheeseburger. I fought the craving and rewarded myself with a big slice of chocolate cake instead.

During the last week of August, I made lunch for Ruth and her husband. They were quite strict about kosher compliance, so this was the ultimate test. We ate in the garden, at the small, round table, which I had covered with a clean white tablecloth, the one which Mamma had embroidered with a rose border. I served the quiche with a green salad, fresh fruit and chocolate cake, which was the only cake I had mastered so far. As I poured the wine, which was kosher, white wine produced in Israel, Ruth smiled at me, while her husband, Ben, nodded his approval.

'Well Sarah, you've done a wonderful job, not just with the lunch but with the garden too.'

'Thank you, Ruth. It's been hard work, but I felt I owed it to Mamma and Papa to keep it up.'

'I'm sure they'd be proud of you. Now enjoy your trip to Vienna and take care of yourself.' I said I would, then spent the next few days frantically shopping for clothes and shoes!

5. Hans

Max leaned back in his chair and smiled at me across the table, in the Café Frauenhuber.

'What's up Hans? You're grinning like an idiot!' I hesitated before answering. Ever since Sarah and I had confirmed the arrangements for her visit in September, I had toyed with the idea of not telling him, but now I thought better of it. *How could I possibly keep it a secret? He's sure to drag it out of me and anyway, it would be a mean thing to do to my friend.*

'Come on Hans, out with it!' I downed the rest of my melange, then blurted it out.

'Sarah's coming to Vienna in September. She wrote to thank me for rescuing her and looking after her in Mayrhofen and I've spoken to her. It's all arranged. Oh, and she wants me to thank you too, for -' Max suddenly leaned forward, eyebrows raised, voice lowered.

'Really? That's great! You must be over the moon. When will she be arriving, and where will she be staying?' I hesitated again, but it was too late to leave out the details. So, I told him what had been arranged. He just sat back again and smiled. I know him so well.

I didn't see Max for several weeks after that, as he was busy performing almost every evening, for the crowds of music-loving tourists in the Orangery. He had a full schedule. I was very busy myself. It was August and my business was flourishing. Joseph was in his element serving customers in the shop and he had a talent for sales. I listened to him extolling the 'unique features and fine craftsmanship' of the silver pieces on display, pieces that my late father and I had designed and created. The orders kept coming in and I often worked well into the evening, trying to keep up.

Sometimes I put aside the contract metalwork and focused instead on my main objective for the next few weeks, which was to create a special silver piece for Sarah, as I had promised. It was intricate, but fun to do. I started with a sketch, just the outline at first, then the finer detail, going over the lines several times until I was satisfied. Then I found a small piece of silver sheet metal, just the right size, and a tiny piece of gold. Working with my blowtorch to melt the metal, and using various tools to form the shapes, I soon became engrossed in the creative process. I still had to meet all the deadlines for the contract work, so I was grateful to Joseph for handling the paperwork and telephone calls, as well as covering the shop so efficiently. The weeks flew by.

During this period, I arranged for Mother's carer to take her for short outings several times a week, as I couldn't take the time and I wanted her to enjoy the fine summer weather. I know Mother was proud of my silverwork and my success, but she still grumbled at the number of hours I put in, not realising, or rather not admitting, the connection between them. As the date for Sarah's arrival approached, I decided it was time to tell Mother all about her.

So, a week before the big day, I took her to Labstelle for lunch. I knew she would love the relaxed atmosphere and the great food. It would be a special treat, so I would tell her then. She would soon be needing a wheelchair as her rheumatoid arthritis was getting worse, but she was able to walk slowly to the restaurant with me, holding on to my arm.

'This is lovely Hans and it's so nice to have some time with you at last.' We were sitting in the restaurant's courtyard, which was full of greenery and sunlight. It was a warm day, so the waiter had found us a table in the shade. I ordered a glass of white wine for each of us and tried to focus on the menu, but I was wondering how Mother would react to the news. She didn't take long to select from the menu, as the waiter approached.

'I would like the Bouillabaisse with Tyrolean Prawns and just a little bread'. As the waiter nodded and smiled, I focused my attention on the menu and ordered my favourite.

'The Austrian Beef Filet please, with potatoes and home-made bacon.' The waiter left and I took a sip of wine. Mother surveyed the other people sitting in the courtyard, frowning slightly and shaking her head. I sensed she was about to comment on the very short skirts and bare shoulders, so I decided to break the news, before the food arrived. Mother listened, quietly nodding, as I told her about the events of the hiking holiday in June, including Sarah's rescue. Finally, I mentioned her imminent visit.

'She must be very special, for you to invite her here.'

'Yes Mother, she is very special and I'm sure you'll agree when you meet her.'

'Well then, we'll see ...' The food arrived and the conversation stopped for a while. When it resumed, it wasn't about Sarah or her visit. Mother preferred to discuss her aches and pains and the doctor's latest recommendations, which included getting a wheelchair. We passed on desserts and coffee, as she was getting tired and beginning to feel the heat, so I paid the waiter and we left. The questions I had expected, about Sarah, never came.

I had been scrambling to meet a big contract deadline for the past few weeks, but I put the finishing touches to Sarah's gift the day before her arrival and placed it in a dark blue velvet pouch, for protection, tying the top with a silver ribbon. That evening I tried to broach the subject of Sarah's arrival again with Mother, but she wasn't interested in discussing it.

The Hotel Domizil, a reputable hotel-guesthouse, was very central, just a two-minute walk from Saint Stephen's Cathedral. I had recommended it to Sarah because of the location. Also, it wasn't quite as expensive as some of the other central hotels. As Sarah would be travelling alone and was unfamiliar with Vienna, I arranged with the hotel for an airport transfer, so she would be picked up at the airport and driven directly to the hotel. I had told Sarah I would meet her at the hotel after she had checked in.

September finally arrived. The big day dawned, bright and clear. I wolfed down my breakfast and then went for a brisk walk to steady my nerves. The flight was on time, so I expected her to arrive at the hotel about 3 pm. I spent the morning in the workshop, ensuring that all the current contracts were up to date and the products shipped. I had already arranged with Joseph for him to take over the shop and any other duties, so I could take the next few days off. Satisfied that all was in order, at 1 pm I went home for lunch, hoping to speak to Mother, but she was out with her carer. I made myself some lunch and then tried to relax, between reading the newspaper, looking at my watch and listening for the telephone.

Sarah rang me at 3:30 to say she had just checked into the hotel, so I suggested we meet in the hotel lobby in an hour, to give her time to unpack and settle into the room. She sounded tired, but happy. As for me, I was ecstatic! I thought carefully about where we might go for dinner and ordered a table for two, then spent the next hour wandering aimlessly around the Stephansplatz, looking in shop windows, but not really seeing anything. The sun was quite warm, but I thought it best to keep my jacket on for meeting her. I didn't want to look too casual, not at first anyway. The little blue pouch was in my jacket pocket. I entered the lobby promptly at 4:30, sat down and waited. I didn't have to wait very long. It just seemed long.

'Hans!'

'Sarah!'

Nothing else was said in that first moment, as she stepped out of the lift and came towards me, a shy smile lighting up her beautiful face. We hugged, then stood looking at each other. After a few breathless moments, I suddenly found my voice, which sounded much too gruff.

'Welcome to Vienna. You look wonderful!' She looked stunning in fact, in a sort of flowing, summery dress and short jacket, open at the front, revealing a low neckline. My eyes took that in, along with her long black hair, smiling lips and those big, dark eyes. Wow!

'Thank you. I can't believe I'm here at last. It's lovely to see you again.'

'Shall we go somewhere for a drink first?'

'Yes, that's a good idea. I'm a bit too tired to go sightseeing right now.'

'We can leave the sightseeing to tomorrow, once you're rested.' I took her hand, which felt like the most natural thing in the world and led her out of the hotel lobby. As we walked through the square, she stumbled a bit, so I held her arm to steady her, and we stopped.

'Are you alright?'

'Yes, dammit! It's these new shoes. They pinch and the heels are too high.'

'Did you bring any other shoes?'

'Yes, I have another pair, with low heels. Are we walking very far right now?'

'No, it's just a bit further along. I've booked a table at the Lamee Rooftop Bar. We can have a drink there and just relax for a while. I've booked somewhere close by for an early dinner.' The lift whisked us up to the bar on the 9th floor, with its panoramic view of Vienna. I had arranged for us to be seated at a small corner table, which gave us some privacy and a clear view of the city. The bar wasn't too crowded at this early hour and the background music was "muted Mozart", so it was easy to talk. Sarah sat down and immediately kicked off her shoes.

'That's a relief! Oh look, what a lovely view of Vienna!'

'Yes, I'm glad we have good weather as it makes all the difference. What would you like?'

'A glass of white wine would be nice. I'll leave it to you.' I signalled the waiter and ordered the drinks, which arrived promptly. It was a warm afternoon, so we took off our jackets. Raising my glass to her, I tried not to stare at the soft curve of her breasts.

'A toast to our reunion and may it be just the beginning of many more reunions.'

'Yes Hans, to our reunion. It was so sweet of you to invite me. Is that St. Stephen's?'

'That's right. It's where I attend Mass. I'll show you around tomorrow.' Sarah quietly sipped her wine, oblivious to the admiring glances from several men at nearby tables.

I was feeling a bit heady, and it wasn't the wine. *Maybe this is what's meant by being drunk with love.* The sun caressed her face and figure, and I had an overwhelming desire to do the same. As she gazed at the view, I felt in my jacket pocket and took out the blue pouch.

'Sarah, this is for you, as promised', as I placed the pouch on the table in front of her.

'What's this? Oh, what a lovely little bag, with a pretty, silver ribbon.' She put down her wine glass and smiled, as she untied the ribbon, opened the pouch and peeped inside.

'Well, aren't you going to take it out?' She carefully lifted the silver bird out of the pouch.

'Hans, it's beautiful! What fine detail on the wings, and it has a tiny gold beak!'

'I'm glad you like it.'

'Like it? I absolutely love it! I'll treasure it always. Thank you!' She placed it so it stood on the table between us, then she leaned over and kissed me gently on the cheek.

Dinner that evening was a candlelit meal, which would have been more romantic if we hadn't been hovered over by several waiters, all wanting a good look at Sarah. We just ordered wine and a main meal, and didn't talk much, just kept smiling at each other. I couldn't wait to get out of there. Sarah was getting tired and hobbling a bit in her new shoes, so I suggested she get an early night and she agreed. We walked back to her hotel, hand in hand, not saying very much, not needing to speak at all. We said goodnight in the lobby and this time it was my turn to kiss her on the cheek. Those lovely lips would have to wait for somewhere a bit more private. *Maybe tomorrow*. When I arrived home that evening Mother was sitting quietly reading, waiting for me.

'You're home earlier than I expected. How is your friend?'

'Sarah's fine. We had a great time, but she's a bit tired. We'll meet again tomorrow morning and I'm taking her sightseeing for the day.'

'That's nice dear, would you hand me my cane? I'm off to bed now.'

That night I lay in bed and stared at the ceiling for a long while, and when I finally dropped off, my dreams were full of sunlit sex and silver birds.

The next day promised to be sunny and warm again. I headed over to Sarah's hotel. She was casually dressed, looking lovely in white slacks and a pink blouse and her hair was tied back loosely with a silver ribbon.

'Is that the ribbon I -'

'Yes, do you like it? It's so pretty I thought I would put it to another use, and I've put the little pouch, with the silver bird, in the safe in my room. I'll take good care of it!'

'Shall we head over to St. Stephen's? It's just around the corner.' She nodded.

'Lead the way. I'm happy to follow wherever you may lead me.' I grinned and took her hand as we left the hotel.

We entered the dim, quiet coolness of the Cathedral, which was devoid of the usual horde of tourists this early in the day, and we moved slowly down the central nave. About halfway down, I made the sign of the cross and genuflected, and we sat down in one of the pews. As we sat there, Sarah looked very solemn as she gazed up at the soaring pillars and the high, vaulted ceiling. I whispered to her as I pointed out some features of the church, my church, where I had been baptised and confirmed. I directed her attention to the gigantic organ, the highly decorated altar with its numerous images of saints and then, finally, the pulpit, with its Gothic detail and lacy, filigree stonework. She looked surprised when I pointed out the stone toads and lizards crawling up the pulpit's staircase balustrade. It was an impressive feature and a source of inspiration for me, capturing my artistic imagination since early childhood.

'Those creatures are symbols of evil, but they are being held off by the stone dog, a symbol of good, and look at the -' but then I noticed she was fidgeting and looking quite pale.

'Can we leave now Hans?' she whispered, leaning against me, 'I'd like to get out in the sunshine'. Sarah's colour returned gradually as we walked around the square. She was happy to window shop, while I tagged along. Then she suddenly turned to face me, eyes bright.

'Hans, will you take me to see your shop? I'd love to see where you work!'

'Of course! I was planning to take you later anyway and it's just down this side street. I'll introduce you to Joseph.'

As we approached my shop, Sara smiled and pointed to the sign above the door, which bore my name and occupation, the same as my late father's: "Hans Kammerer, Metallkunst", and right next to the sign was an oval, silver plaque, bearing a stylised replica of a bird in flight. As we entered the shop, Joseph was serving a customer, so we stood quietly just inside the entrance and waited until the customer left, carrying a small parcel, nodding and smiling at us as he left. Sarah was admiring the items on display, so I took her hand and walked her over to the counter, where Joseph stood grinning at us.

'Joseph, I'd like you to meet my very special friend, Sarah.'

'I'm delighted to meet you at last Sarah! Welcome to Vienna!'

'Thank you, Joseph. It's lovely to be here and Hans has been just wonderful!' Two more customers entered the shop, so I steered Sarah through to my workshop at the rear. I heard her gasp when she saw my hefty blowtorch, large array of tools and scraps of silver metal of various shapes and sizes, some with sharp edges, scattered over my wooden workbench.

'Isn't this dangerous work?'

'It could be, but I'm very careful and I don't take any chances.' I showed her my thick goggles and brown leather apron, which were hanging on a peg, then I put them on to show her, along with my protective gloves. 'I never work without my protective equipment.'

'Good! I'd be worried about you otherwise. What are these lovely pieces on the shelf?'

'They're not quite finished yet. This is a silver tray and six napkin rings. I'm making them for a customer who wants to surprise his wife on her birthday. He wants me to engrave them all with a flower and leaf design. I always start any intricate work by sketching some designs first. This is an essential step and it's where my art courses come in handy. Here's my sketchbook.'

'Oh, here's where you've sketched the designs for my silver bird! You're quite an artist!'

'Thank you. Here are some sketches I did for a small silver crucifix for another client. She wanted it for her mother's rosary, and here are the drawings and designs for a silver chalice, which I engraved with a dove of peace. I've just shipped it to the Vatican.' She glanced at the sketches and designs, nodded, then flipped through the remaining pages of my sketchbook.

'Sarah, now you've seen where I work, let's go for some Viennese coffee.' We waved to Joseph on the way out. He was busy talking on the telephone. He grinned and waved back.

Sarah was very quiet as we sat sipping our melanges in the Café Pruckel and I couldn't tempt her to try the apple strudel. Maybe it was just as well, as we'd be heading over to the Naschmarkt next, for an early lunch and a real feast for the senses. She finished her coffee.

'Hans, how is Max? Will I get to see him soon or is he too busy performing?'

'Max is fine as far as I know. I haven't seen him for weeks, but I'll give him a call.'

6. Sarah

Hans was very quiet as we walked to the market, and I suspected it had to do with Max.

'Are you and Max still good friends?'

'Of course! Why do you ask?'

'Oh, nothing really. It's just that--'

'Sarah, I told you I'd get in touch, and we'll meet up with him soon ... ok?'

For the first time since I arrived in Vienna, I began to see another side of Hans, a slightly more impatient side. It surprised me, but it made him more human somehow, and God knows, I'm far from perfect myself! *How could I not love him? He's a talented artist and silversmith, he's so good to me, and so incredibly handsome. It's hard to believe I could be so lucky!* I gave his hand a little squeeze and he let go, slipping it around my waist and pulling me close. It was unexpected, so I trembled a little as I leaned against him and savoured his manly scent. His face was so close to mine, I closed my eyes and held my breath ... but then we just walked on.

As soon as we arrived at the market, we were quickly surrounded by the steamy atmosphere, the smells of cooking food, the blindingly bright colours of the fruits and vegetables, and the loud, competing, almost cacophonous, shouts of the multi-ethnic, haggling traders in the stalls. It was so crowded we had to elbow our way through. We passed stalls with dried fruits, nuts and wafts of fresh falafel. It reminded me of a Middle Eastern market, and I began to feel quite at home. It was a multicultural microclimate with Turks, Greeks, Indians and Chinese, together with the local Viennese.

'Sarah, you must try some pork dumplings or how about a kebab?' Hans had stopped at one of the snack bars and was surveying the sizzling food selections, while simultaneously looking for an empty table, so we could sit down. 'There's an empty table. Let's grab it.' I looked at the menu. The pork dumplings were out of the question, as were the kebabs and there was no salad.

'Hans, I'd just like some falafel and a green salad, but you go ahead if you'd like to eat here.'

'Nonsense! We'll go and get your falafel and green salad. I'm sure I'll find something too.'

We eventually found a table in the Turkish restaurant and Hans ordered two plates of hot falafel, which came served in hefty pita pockets, crammed with vegetable salad and hummus.

'Well, there's your falafel and salad, all together inside the pita. Are you a vegetarian?'

'I'm trying to be, but it's not so easy sometimes, depending on who I'm eating with.'

'I can imagine. I must admit I'm a meat and potatoes man myself, but this is pretty good.' We polished off the pitas, then tried the Turkish coffee, which was so strong I couldn't finish it.

'Let's get out of here.' Hans grabbed my hand and led me away from the noisy, bustling crowd. The afternoon was spent wandering around the Hofburg, which Hans explained was the official residence of the Austrian Head of State. He was explaining the history of the place as we walked. However, it was such a gigantic complex, with numerous buildings and courtyards spread over many acres, that I felt overwhelmed. I couldn't concentrate and my eyes were getting blurry.

'Why are you limping? Is it your shoes again?' We stopped.

'Was I limping? These shoes are fine. I think I'm just getting tired of all the walking.'

'I've been such an idiot to drag you around like this. I just wanted to show you Vienna.'

'And I do appreciate it Hans, it's so interesting. I'll be fine after I've rested for a while.'

We left the Hofburg area and headed back towards the Stephansplatz, just a few streets away.

'Let's go in here. You need to sit down and this time you must try the apple strudel.' We were in yet another café. I tried the strudel to please him. It was tart and flaky and it revived me.

'You were right, Hans. It's delicious! Now, tell me about your mother. How is she?'

'She has rheumatoid arthritis, which is progressive, so she's struggling quite a bit now and her doctor has recommended a wheelchair. She has a carer, who comes in every day and that helps, as I'm so busy with work that I can't spend much time with her. The carer takes her out regularly.'

'I would love to meet her.' Hans seemed to consider this but took a few minutes to answer.

'Yes, I want you to meet her. I'll arrange for us to have lunch together before you leave.' We sat there, quietly relaxing and watching the steady stream of people crossing the busy plaza, through the large café windows. I felt a bit guilty, like I was holding him back.

'Hans, I'm sorry I've been such a party-pooper, what with my feeling tired all the time.'

'Don't be silly, it's my fault for dragging you here, there and everywhere. You don't have to see everything. The main thing is, we're spending time together. I'll ease up the pace a bit.'

True to his word, the rest of the day was very relaxing. We just strolled around one of the parks, stopping to sit on a bench in the late afternoon sunlight, with my head resting on his shoulder. He gently kissed the top of my head and as I lifted my face to look up at him, his warm lips came down on mine and stayed there for a lingering, breath-taking moment that I can still feel. There must have been people passing by, but we were lost in a silent, timeless world of our own. We could have stayed in that embrace forever, except for a small boy chasing a ball, which landed in my lap, causing a fit of giggles in the boy and an apology from his frazzled mother.

'Well, darling, do you think perhaps we could find somewhere a bit more private later?'

'I hope so ...' was all I could say.

'Where would you like to have dinner? How about a vegetarian restaurant?'

'No, you're a carnivore and you don't have to cater to me. I'm sure I'll find something to eat.'

'In that case, let's see if we can find a restaurant near your hotel', as he squeezed my hand.

I don't remember much about the restaurant that evening, as I was too keyed up and couldn't eat much anyway. I do recall Hans polishing off a huge bowl of goulash though, along with thick slabs of bread. After dinner we strolled the short distance back to my hotel, his arm around my waist. The receptionist smiled and nodded as we entered and we smiled back, trying to look nonchalant as we waited for the lift. As soon as the lift doors had closed, he kissed me again, more urgently this time and I responded eagerly, so when the doors opened at my floor and an elderly couple got in, coughing discreetly, we wrenched ourselves apart, red-faced, and rushed out, giggling nervously. My hand was shaking so badly, I fumbled with the room key card, then dropped it. Hans picked it up, inserted it into the lock and opened the door. He steered me inside, closed the door, placed the key card on the TV stand and turned to face me.

Without a word, he caressed my face, untied the silver ribbon and stroked my hair. He pulled me close so I could feel his body hardening against me, then his hands moved to the buttons of my blouse. After an initial struggle with them, he finally undid them all and, as my bra seemed to pose another challenge for him,

I unhooked it. His hands quickly found my breasts and his warm, caressing touch made me gasp. I closed my eyes as his mouth moved slowly over my neck, then my shoulders, then my breasts and a few moments later my clothes were lying in a heap on the floor, and I was frantically undressing him on the bed. We made love with a passion I'd never felt before, not even with Daniel. This was special because he was special, and I felt like we fit together perfectly and belonged together forever.

When our passion was spent, he dozed off and I lay there, just gazing at him. His body was lean and firm and with his fair, curly hair and handsome face he reminded me of a god, though I couldn't say which one and I didn't care. I kissed him gently, then buried my face in the soft, fuzzy hair on his chest. We both slept for several hours in the quiet darkness of the room. When I woke with a start, Hans was pulling on his clothes. He bent down to kiss me, then sat on the bed and put on his shoes.

'Where are you going? Why don't you stay?' I mumbled.

'Sarah darling, I must go home now. I can't leave Mother alone at night.' I felt like saying something sarcastic, but knew I shouldn't, so I just rolled over and buried my face in the pillow.

'Look, I'm sorry darling. I'll call you in the morning and we'll spend another day together', and with that he left me lying there. I felt abandoned. I stared at the ceiling for ages, thinking about the passionate love we'd shared together and wondering how he could leave me so casually after that. *Surely his mother could survive the night without him. If she's that bad, why doesn't he arrange for a live-in carer? He's a successful businessman and shouldn't be living with his mother. Well, I'm not going to play second fiddle to her, even if she's an invalid!* I felt my anger rising to a fever pitch, until I screamed and pounded the pillow where he'd been sleeping like a god.

The next morning, the loud jangling of the room telephone woke me from a restless sleep. Groaning, I rolled over and checked the time on my travel alarm ... 10 am. *It's probably Hans and I don't really feel like talking to him right now. On the other hand, I must find out exactly where I stand with him, especially after last night. This obsession with his mother is ridiculous!* So I let it ring a few times before lifting the receiver and then I just waited for him to speak first.

'Sarah? It's Max.' I sat bolt upright on the edge of the bed and took a deep breath.

'Max! What a lovely surprise! Did Hans tell you I was here?'

'I haven't spoken to him recently, but I've known about your visit for a few weeks, and he told me where you'd be staying. Welcome to Vienna!'

'Thank you! I'll be here a few more days, so it would be great to see you, if you have time.'

'Yes, that's why I'm calling. I'm performing tomorrow evening at the Orangery with the Schönbrunn Palace Orchestra. It's a typical Viennese programme, Mozart and Strauss. If you're interested, I can get tickets for you and Hans. We could all get together afterwards for a drink.'

'That sounds great! I'd love to see ... I'd love to hear you perform and I love Mozart!'

'Right then, I'll call Hans now and confirm it with him and I look forward to seeing you!'

'Thank you so much for calling Max. I'm really looking forward to seeing you tomorrow!' Hearing Max's voice after so long, along with the prospect of seeing him again soon, cheered me, so my mood was much improved by the time Hans called me a half hour later.

'Good morning. I've just heard from Max.' He spoke quietly and sounded a bit hesitant.

'Yes, he called me too. He's getting us tickets for the concert tomorrow evening!'

'If you really want to go, perhaps we can spend tomorrow afternoon touring the Schönbrunn Palace and gardens, so we won't have far to walk when the evening concert begins.'

'Yes, I do want to go and that's a great idea.' I didn't fancy chasing all over Vienna again.

'I'll pick you up in an hour. We're having lunch with Mother today.'

My stomach was churning as I rushed to shower, blow-dry my hair, apply makeup and get dressed before Hans arrived. *What can I wear to impress her ... and why do I care?* Considering my feeling of resentment towards her last night, I was nervous about meeting her and wondered if my resentment would show. I decided to wear my pale blue linen dress with my comfortable black sandals and carry my small, black clutch bag. Classic, understated elegance was the look I wanted to achieve and the full-length mirror in the room told me I'd succeeded. When I stepped out of the lift in the lobby and saw Hans look me over, grinning that schoolboy grin, I was oozing confidence and knew I'd be able to handle his mother, no problem.

'Darling, you look wonderful, as usual!' He kissed my cheek, slipped his arm around my waist, hugged me tightly and steered me towards the hotel entrance. 'I have a taxi waiting outside, so we'll go and collect Mother first, then continue in the taxi to the restaurant.' The taxi didn't have far to go and pulled up outside an impressive, three-storey building, with a uniformed doorman.

'Is this where you live?'

'Yes, Mother and I have an apartment on the top floor. Wait here, I won't be long.'

The doorman smiled and nodded, holding the door open as Hans entered. As I waited in the taxi, my nervousness returned.

Whatever image I had formed of Hans's mother was soon erased, when she emerged with him a few minutes later. I had imagined a frail, slightly stooped old woman with white hair and drab, old-fashioned clothes. The woman who was being escorted to the taxi was the exact opposite! Frau Kammerer couldn't have been much more than 50, quite tall, with short, styled, blonde hair, discreet touches of makeup and a flawless complexion. Her cream-coloured, tailored suit was paired with a navy-blue blouse, matching shoes and handbag. She was the image of mature sophistication, which did nothing to alleviate my nervousness. Her posture was perfect, but she walked slowly, as if in pain, and leaned heavily on Hans's arm. He helped her into the back of the taxi, next to me, while he sat in front with the driver. He turned to face us.

'Mother, I'd like you to meet Sarah ... Sarah, this is my mother.'

'I'm very pleased to meet you, my dear,' she said, extending her hand and looking me over.

'I'm pleased to meet you too, Frau Kammerer,' as I shook her hand and tried to calm my nerves. I couldn't help noticing her silver earrings and matching silver brooch, both in a delicate rosebud and leaf design, and wondering if Hans had made them for her. *Why does this thought bother me?* As the taxi set off, there was a mere suggestion of her perfume, which I didn't recognise, but it was very light, with floral top notes ... roses? *Damn! I forgot to wear my perfume and jewellery. Maybe it's just as well. I wouldn't want to compete with her!* Hans was chatting to the driver, but there was no chatting in the back seat, as we both just looked out of the windows.

The taxi soon pulled up outside the Hotel Sacher Wien, across from the Vienna State Opera. Hans paid the driver and jumped out to help us both out of the back seat. His mother immediately took his arm and they walked together slowly, into the hotel, leaving me to follow behind, feeling just a trifle irritated. The elegant dining room was busy but welcoming and we were promptly shown to our table. The opulent décor included burgundy damask walls, adorned with large paintings, plush seating and glittering chandeliers. Hans explained to me that this was the home of the famous "Sachertorte" and suggested that we might order it for dessert. When the menu arrived, it looked blurry to me, probably due to the glare from the chandeliers. After Hans had ordered a bottle of wine for us, I asked him to translate the main menu items for me.

'Darling, the English translation is just underneath the German description for each dish.'

'Well, I'm having trouble focusing, because of the chandeliers, so can you read it for me?'

'There are a few vegetarian dishes, so I'll read those for you.' He was frowning a bit as he read. After we had ordered our meals, Hans's mother fixed her steady gaze on me.

'Are you a vegetarian my dear? That must limit you quite a bit.' *Why does she keep staring?*

'I don't feel limited at all. There are lots of other, healthy alternatives, and I have no interest in eating slaughtered animals or dead fish anymore. Also, I'm Jewish, so I prefer kosher. I just thought you should know.' The words flowed out of me in a sudden torrent, as complete silence descended on our little table. The waiter approached and poured the wine.

Hans's mother raised her eyebrows, frowned, then looked down at the table and fiddled with her cutlery. Hans just stared at me, ashen faced. As for me, I felt surprisingly smug, and I basked in being the centre of attention at last. There wouldn't be any toasts this time, so I immediately took a large sip of wine and then another, glancing casually around the room. Hans finally found his voice, turning to his mother and asking, quietly, if she was comfortable. She was fidgeting in her seat, but she nodded and took a sip of wine. Thankfully the food arrived soon afterwards, so we all had something to do. I tucked into my eggplant, truffles and cheese, which was truly delicious, feeling a huge sense of relief to have finally had the courage to tell them. *It's the truth, so there's no sense pretending I'm something I'm not and they'll just have to accept me for who I am.* Frau Kammerer was picking delicately at her sea trout. Hans kept glancing at me, as he ate his venison.

'Would anyone like dessert?' The waiter was smiling at me, looking me over. I smiled back.

'Yes, I would love to try your famous Sachertorte!' I was in the mood for a chocolate fix.

'Not for me, thank you. I'm watching my weight. I'll just have a melange.' *She's slim enough!*

'Yes, I'll have the Sachertorte too.' Hans replied, then he turned to chat to his mother, who was pointing to one of the paintings on the wall. *So much for me being the centre of attention.* The Sachertorte, with a thick dollop of cream, melted in my mouth, rounding off an excellent, interesting meal.

As we left the restaurant, Hans and his mother walked slowly ahead again, arm in arm, with me following, like a lonely shadow, behind them. Hans turned to me, frowning, as his mother climbed into the back seat of the taxi. His face was pale as he touched my arm and whispered.

'Sarah, we need to talk.' It made me feel like a naughty child. I just nodded, then climbed into the taxi, next to his mother. Another silent journey, looking out of our respective windows. Frau Kammerer's goodbye to me was brief. There was no smile or eye contact. Hans escorted her into the apartment building, then took ages to come back out, as I waited in the taxi.

7. Hans

Mother said nothing to me as I helped her back into the apartment. Her face said everything.

'You're as white as a sheet Mother. Sit down here and I'll get you a glass of water.' She slumped into the armchair, and I rushed to the kitchen. When I got back, she was sitting ramrod-straight, tight-lipped and shaking so badly I had to put the glass on the side table. Her voice, when she finally spoke, was like the slow rumble of thunder, just before an approaching storm.

'That young woman is not for you. She's rude and insulting.'

'I don't think she meant to be rude or insulting. She was just being honest with us.'

'Don't make excuses for her!' The thunder was getting louder.

'I'm not!'

'Yes, you are, because she's attractive and you think you're in love.'

'Sarah's beautiful but she's intelligent too. She's studying to be a music teacher.'

'Huh!' She grunted, tossing her head in contempt.

'You've only just met her, so you don't know her like I do.'

'Hans, you've been in love before, a couple of times as I recall, and look what happened.'

'That wasn't love, not like this ...'

'I didn't care for them either. You're a poor judge of character. Trust me!' I was pacing the room and decided to confront her with the main reason for her objections.

'Mother, you're not being fair. Is it because she's Jewish? It was a surprise for me too, but that doesn't change how I feel.' She turned away from my steady gaze and I knew I was right. After a moment's pregnant silence, she turned back to face me again, her eyes and voice softer now.

'Hans, if your relationship develops the way you seem to want, it will be difficult for you both. I've seen it happen before with one of my friends and I don't want you to suffer like that, because I care about you.' She took a sip of water. The thunder had abated but I wasn't totally convinced.

'I'd better get back to her now, the taxi's waiting and she'll be wondering. I'll see you later.'

Sarah was fiddling with her hair, silently turning her back to me as I re-entered the taxi.

'I'm sorry it took so long to get Mother settled. Are you ok?'

'Your mother has made it quite clear she doesn't like me. Well, the feeling is mutual!'

'Sarah, she doesn't even know you and you mustn't take it so personally.'

'Personally! How else am I to take it? Is it because I'm Jewish?' I hesitated, which said it all. Her back was still turned and as I reached out, trying to take her hand, she pulled it away.

'If I had told you when we met, you would have felt differently about me.'

'No, I wouldn't! I may be a Catholic and my faith is very important to me but--'

'Please tell me the truth Hans! How do you feel about me now?' She had finally turned to face me, her dark eyes intense and questioning, her lips so close, I decided to show her. It was a tender kiss that was meant to convince her of my feelings, but she pushed me away.

'What's wrong now?' I could see the taxi driver in the rear-view mirror, smiling to himself.

'How could you abandon me last night, after we ... to hurry home to your mother? She's not that ill, from what I could see. I think she just wants to keep you tied to her apron strings!'

'Sarah, you don't realise how bad the pain gets sometimes, but let's not argue over this.' The taxi had pulled up outside the hotel, so I paid the driver, and we entered the lobby.

'It's only 3 pm Sarah, so what would you like to do? Maybe we could--'

'Hans, I'd like to go back to my room for a bit, by myself, then go shopping in the plaza.'

'Of course. If that's what you want. I'll go and see how Joseph is doing. What time would you like to meet up for dinner? There's a vegetarian restaurant in the --'

'I'll probably be tired from shopping, so I'll just order room service and get an early night.'

'Oh, I was hoping --' Then I noticed her face was quite pale and drawn so I let it go. 'I'll call you tomorrow then and we'll head over to Schönbrunn.'

'Yes, it will be great to see Max again and I'm looking forward to the concert. Thank you for the lovely lunch today.' Then she gave me a quick hug, much too quick, and pushed the button on the lift. After the lift door had closed, I stood there, rooted to the spot, for several minutes, struggling with a perplexing mix of feelings. I was disappointed and frustrated, but I was also concerned for her.

Sleep was a long time coming that night. I grappled with my love for Sarah, which was as strong as ever, and my love and duty to Mother, which was pulling me in the opposite direction. It was tearing me apart; because I knew they were both so strong-willed, there would be no chance of a softening on either side. I would have to decide between them, or at least try to call a truce, before Sarah returned to London the day after tomorrow.

Mother woke me at 6am, stumbling around in the kitchen, trying to make tea. I knew the kettle was too heavy for her painful fingers to lift, so I got up. I felt grumpy, from a combination of too little sleep and too much frustration. I hadn't told Sarah what time I'd be calling her, so I decided to go back to bed and catch forty winks and then have a quiet morning at home. I'd give Sarah a call after lunch, as we'd be together all afternoon at Schönbrunn Palace and then in the evening, at the concert in the Orangery. Mother had other ideas when I told her the plan.

'But Hans, I was hoping you'd take me to my doctor's appointment later this afternoon.'

'I'm sorry Mother, but I promised Sarah we'd tour Schönbrunn. She only has today, as she's returning home tomorrow, and we have tickets for the concert at the Orangery tonight.'

'I see. I'll have to call the taxi then. You look very pale. I'm sorry I woke you so early.'

'It's not your fault. I'm going to take a nap now and then we can have lunch together.'

Peace reigned during lunch, as we both avoided discussing Sarah, who would be leaving soon anyway. There was no answer in Sarah's hotel room when I called, so I decided to walk over and look for her. She was probably shopping again, so I headed for the Stephansplatz and wandered around there for a bit, but there was no sign of her. *Maybe she's back at the hotel now.* As I walked into the lobby, I saw her sitting in the lounge, looking relaxed and happy, with a glass of wine ... and Max! *How long has he been here? Was he with her last night? So that's why she didn't want to meet me for dinner. He must have called her at some point and asked to see her alone ... the rat!* Sarah saw me first and her hand was shaking slightly as she put down her wine glass.

'Oh Hans, look who's here! We just bumped into each other in the plaza this morning.'

'Hans, buddy, good to see you! I've been keeping Sarah company for a while.' Then, as I stood there in front of them, silently fuming, he drained his wine glass and jumped up.

'Look, I must run ... rehearsals this afternoon. I'll see you this evening. Here are the tickets. Meet me in the foyer after the concert.' Then he swept out of the lounge. Sarah's eyes were bright, watching him leave, and at that moment I feared I was losing her.

'I decided to do some last-minute shopping in the plaza, before my flight leaves tomorrow afternoon, and suddenly Max appeared, on his way over with the tickets.' She flushed.

'So, what did you buy? I don't see any parcels or shopping bags.' I had to know the truth.

'I didn't find anything suitable, so I just did some browsing ... lovely shops!'

'Where did you have lunch?' I sat down close to her, making sure our thighs were touching.

'In one of the cafés in the plaza. Why are you grilling me?' She moved slightly, then stood up.

'Where are you going?'

'Just back to my room to change, if we're going to the concert tonight. I won't be long.'

'I'm coming with you.' There was no way I was letting her out of my sight.

I'm not proud of my behaviour that afternoon. Even though all I had were suspicions, I still felt betrayed by Sarah, who'd been acting strangely, and Max, who was supposed to be my best friend. As soon as we entered her room, I grabbed her arms and swung her round to face me.

'Was Max here with you last night? Tell me the truth Sarah!'

'No! He wasn't here! We only met this morning. Let me go!' Even though I had to admit I believed her, my jealousy and my passion for her got the better of me and I pulled her close, kissed her roughly, and pushed her onto the bed.

'Hans, what are you doing?' She looked surprised and I suddenly felt ashamed.

'I'm sorry Sarah, I didn't mean to ... I just get so jealous. Please forgive me.'

She lay there silently for a few moments then sat up and pulled me down onto the bed, kissing me and sliding her hands inside my shirt, like she was excited by my jealousy, and I was forgiven. Our mutual passions soon overtook us, and I felt her body responding, rising to meet mine. We spent the next couple of hours wrapped up in each other, our naked bodies glistening with sweat, the sheets beneath us moist and slippery as our passions undulated in perfect rhythm. We dozed, then devoured each other again, until we fell back, exhausted and content.

Afterwards, we showered together, giggling like children as we rubbed the slippery soap all over each other, lingering over the sweet spots and pausing several times to kiss, as if time was running out ... which it was. I was trying hard not to think about her leaving tomorrow.

'Will this be suitable for the concert tonight?' She was twirling around in her flowery dress, the one with the low-cut neckline. 'I have a plain black one, which is a bit more elegant.' I could just imagine Max looking her over, whatever she wore, undressing her with his eyes.

'No, that one is fine, but maybe you should wear your short jacket over it. It will be a bit cooler tonight.' The real reason for suggesting the jacket had nothing to do with the weather.

It was late afternoon by the time we arrived at Schönbrunn. We did a guided tour of the Palace, so Sarah could admire the beautiful rooms, furniture and artwork and learn about the history. She smiled when she heard about six-year-old Mozart's debut performance for the Empress Maria Theresia in the Hall of Mirrors, and how he jumped into her lap afterwards.

As we strolled around the Palace Gardens, I noticed she was limping again, more like listing to one side. I was starting to worry about her and suggested we sit down and rest for a while.

'Sarah, you've been having trouble walking a few times since you arrived. What's wrong?'

'To be honest, I don't know. It's not my shoes and it's probably nothing, just some weakness from when I sprained my ankle in Mayrhofen.' She looked unconcerned, shrugging it off.

'Maybe, but it might be a good idea to get checked by a doctor, when you get home.' I also remembered how her eyes went blurry in the Sacher Restaurant, and she couldn't read the menu. I wondered if there might be a connection, but I didn't mention it, as I didn't want to upset her.

'What a glorious view of the gardens and palace and the rooftops of Vienna!' We were sitting at a window table in the Gloriette Café, at the top of the hill, enjoying our wine and a light meal of potato pancakes and grilled vegetables. The setting sun cast its golden glow over the view. She leaned back in her chair, closing her eyes, allowing the sun to light up her face and the soft curves of her figure and I was suddenly breathless again. The people sitting at nearby tables seemed to be admiring her too. *I wonder if she realises the effect she has on people ... she's the centre of attention wherever we go ... no wonder I get jealous ... her flowing, raven-black hair, those big, dark, doe eyes, soft pink lips and creamy skin ... she looks like a goddess ... I should sketch her!*

'Do we have time for dessert?' Her down-to-earth question broke into my fanciful thoughts.

'No darling. We don't want to be late. Let's head over to the Orangery now.' As we walked, I noticed her left foot was dragging a bit. She seemed aware of it as she kept looking down, so I didn't say anything, but I decided to do some research about her symptoms.

The Orangery was alive with the subdued chatter of the crowd. I held Sarah's hand as we negotiated the busy foyer and found our seats. They were in the front row, dead centre.

'I guess Max wanted to make sure we could see him properly.' I was joking, but silently glad, as Sarah's eyes might get blurry again. I gave her the programme to read, watching her closely, but she just glanced at the people around her. The bustling, rustling audience was finally settled, and the background lights began their changing, pastel-coloured show. Sarah watched silently. When the lights dimmed and the silver stars started whirling around the room, she gasped and smiled. There was a burst of applause as the spotlight fell on the orchestra and the conductor entered.

Max looked directly at us, gave a brief, serious nod, then turned his eyes to the conductor. He was sitting in the second violin section, next to the concertmaster. The conductor bowed to the audience, swiftly turned and raised his baton and the orchestra sprang to life with Mozart's Symphony No. 40. It was a lively opener and a showcase for the singing violins. I have always been amazed at Max's musical talent, how seriously he approaches his career and how hard he works. His professional persona sometimes seems at odds with his off-duty, fun-loving behaviour.

During the interval, Sarah was very quiet, and spent a long time in the Ladies.

'Just powdering my nose,' she laughed. The concert was a combination of orchestral music, opera and dance, performed to Mozart and Strauss. Whenever I glanced at Sarah, her eyes were focused on Max, even while the opera singers and ballet dancers were performing.

As we waited for him in the foyer afterwards, I asked her what she thought of the concert.

'Max is such a wonderful musician, isn't he? He's so serious when he's performing.'

'Yes, he's very good, but I meant how did you like the concert.'

'Oh, it was lovely Hans! I love Mozart and this is such a beautiful place.' She kept glancing around expectantly until Max finally appeared, large as life, jacket slung over his shoulder, shirt collar unbuttoned, grinning as he strode towards us, carrying his violin case.

'Sarah! You're looking lovely!' He threw his jacket on a chair, carefully put the case down and hugged her. It was a bear hug, and a few seconds longer than needed, then he slapped me on the back. 'How are you buddy? You lucky devil! What did you both think of the concert?' Sarah was effusive with her praise, so I didn't need to say anything. As she showered him with compliments, he was smiling and looking her over, undressing her with his eyes, just as I had predicted.

'Let's grab a taxi and head back to the Stephansplatz. We can have a drink and relax.'

The three of us crowded into the back seat of a taxi. Sarah was sitting between us, chatting away to Max about the concert. I grabbed her hand and started caressing it gently, but she didn't seem to notice. All I could think about was how much I needed her all to myself tonight, and how much we needed to sort out, before she left me tomorrow. We found a bar near Sarah's hotel.

'So, you've decided to become a music teacher. Which instrument do you play?'

'I play the piano. I've been playing since I was six years old. My mother played. She taught me until I started formal lessons, and my father had a wonderful voice, a strong baritone. He was always singing, especially during Shabbat.'

'You're Jewish!'

'Yes, my parents brought me up in the Jewish traditions, which I still try to follow.'

'That's great! It can't be easy, with so much prejudice around still.'

'No, it isn't easy,' with a brief glance at me, 'but I'm proud of my heritage. My parents are gone now, but I live in a close-knit, supportive, Jewish community. My grandfather and many other relatives were victims of the Holocaust.' I downed my drink and immediately ordered another. Max kept peppering Sarah with questions, and she kept answering, blushing, smiling at him, telling him things I never knew, because I had never asked.

'Are you a Catholic Max? Like Hans?'

'No, I'm nothing really. I mean I'm not religious, not like you and Hans.' I was drinking too much, feeling more and more irritated and wishing Max would shut up and leave us alone. Sarah seemed oblivious to my presence. When I knocked my glass over, spilling the contents over the table, she just stared at me, shaking her head. The waiter rushed to help, and Max stood up.

'Hans, buddy, you've had a few too many. We'd better see Sarah back to her hotel.' He paid the bill and helped me to stand up. I was staggering across the plaza, leaning on him, trying to grab Sarah's hand and Max was clutching his precious violin case, so we must have looked like quite a trio! In the lobby Sarah took my hand, squeezed it and kissed me lightly on the cheek. My heart sank.

'Goodnight, Hans. Get some sleep and call me tomorrow morning. We can talk then. Thank you for everything Max! It was a lovely evening. I hope we can meet up again soon.' He hugged her, another bloody bear hug, then took out a pen and one of his cards and dealt me the final blow.

'Sarah, I'll be touring with the orchestra in December. We'll be in London for a few days, performing at the Royal Festival Hall. I'll call you with the details ... what's your number?'

8. Sarah

It was my last night in Vienna. I never thought I'd be sleeping alone, but it was probably for the best, considering my increasingly confused feelings about Hans and the fact he was very drunk. His mother would be expecting him home too, which would put yet another damper on things! Our passionate lovemaking in the afternoon was fun, but he scared me a little at first, with his angry accusations about me and Max and the wild look in his eyes when he grabbed me and pushed me onto the bed. At the time I was flattered by his jealousy, but I had to admit it was having a relaxed drink with Max in the lounge, and the thought of seeing him at the concert that evening which excited me, more than the lovemaking with Hans.

What's happening to me? I thought I was in love with Hans. Maybe I've just been blinded by his boyish good looks and his overwhelming feelings for me, which now seem more like a teenage infatuation than real love. I admire his artistic talent, his success in business and his generous nature ... my beautiful silver bird ... but as a potential life partner he's weak and a mamma's boy. Oh God, it's hopeless! I need a strong man who'll be a good match for me, who'll understand me, share my interests, be free to love and take care of me ... someone like Max!

I lay staring at the ceiling, thinking about his performance at the concert and seeing again the serious expression on his tanned, attractive face, his dark hair gleaming under the lights, his eyes half closed as he seemed to be lost in the music. He was caressing his violin with those long, supple fingers, as the tempo and volume increased, building up to that final, climactic crescendo. The overall effect inflamed my imagination. I could see us making music together.

It's always been Hans and he saved my life, but the past few days have revealed things about him that make me uncomfortable ... like his unhealthy obsession with his mother, his tendency to sulk and drink too much and his quick temper. I'll have to break it off. Max wants to see me in London! He'll be there for a few days with the orchestra, so we'll have some time to get to know each other and who knows ... I smiled to myself, reached over and turned off the light.

I woke early the next morning and ordered breakfast in my room. As I sat sipping my orange juice and nibbling at my cheese roll, I wondered what to say to Hans when he telephoned. I was still waiting to hear from him by mid-morning. I had finished packing, so I wandered down to the lobby to stretch my legs and check the time of the airport transfer. The concierge said it would be leaving in an hour. As I turned to go back to my room I came face to face with Hans, unshaven, dishevelled and as white as a sheet.

'Sarah! I had to see you before you go. Can we talk ... please?'

'You look shattered, and I'm not surprised, with the amount you had to drink last night. Come up to my room, but we don't have much time. I'm leaving in an hour.' We took the crowded lift, entered my room silently and sat together on the bed. I knew I'd have to be honest with him.

'Please forgive me Sarah. I've been an idiot and I'm not proud of my behaviour.'

'Hans, apart from your behaviour yesterday you've been very good to me. I'm thrilled with the beautiful silver bird you made for me, and I'll always treasure it. I'm not angry with you, I'm just trying to understand you and your obsession with your mother. She can't seem to accept me, and she probably never will, but I can't change who I am.'

'Of course not! You don't have to change for anyone!'

'You've taken me to your church and your workshop, taken me around your city and introduced me to your mother. But you've never asked me about my family background, my Jewish faith, my music or my career ... all the things that make me who I am. I feel like you're just infatuated with how I look and how we made love.' Hans turned suddenly to face me.

'Sarah darling, you're wrong about my just being infatuated. I love you madly! I always have, from the first time I saw you at that restaurant in Mayrhofen. I've been so focused on trying to impress you I've forgotten to focus on getting to know more about you and your life.'

'I thought I loved you too Hans, but there are too many strikes against us. There's the difference in our religion, your mother's objections, the fact we live so far apart, the fact I'm vegetarian and you're a carnivore ...' I smiled at that one, but Hans wasn't smiling.

'Sarah, none of that should matter if we really love each other. We can make it work.'

'You think so? I'm not convinced. I'm sorry, but I must get down to the lobby now.' We stood up and embraced, then kissed for one last time, a tender kiss that brought tears to my eyes. Hans carried my suitcase as we returned to the lobby, and as we sat in the lounge to wait, I felt a strange tingling in the nerves of my hands, like an electric shock. I gasped.

'What's the matter?'

'It's my hands. They feel like there's an electric current running through them.'

'Promise me you'll see your doctor for a check-up as soon as you get home!' He took my hands in his, gently massaging them. The strange feeling passed as suddenly as it had started.

'Yes, I promise to make an appointment and I'll let you know what the doctor says.'

'Good! In the meantime, take care of yourself!'

'Here's the airport express. Thanks again Hans for everything, the silver bird, the sightseeing, the meals, the ... lovemaking ... everything!' One last hug and I left him standing there.

The flight home was an irritating, discordant mix of clattering aisle trolleys, overly friendly fellow passengers and crying babies, as I struggled with my mixed emotions over the break-up.

Poor Hans, I know he's devastated, and he really does seem to care about me, but it had to be done. I know it would never work and it would be cruel to let him think otherwise. It's been quite an eventful week ... one I'll never forget. And then there's Max. God he's so ... perfect for me. But I'll keep my promise to let Hans know the result of my doctor's appointment. No need to cut him off so drastically, but I must be firm with him about us not seeing each other anymore. I wonder what's wrong with me ... all these strange symptoms ... I'm a bit scared to find out.

The rest of the flight was spent dozing and dreaming of Max, while my silver bird, nestling in its dark blue pouch, was kept safely in my handbag.

As soon as I entered the house, I took out the silver bird, stroked it gently and placed it carefully on top of the piano, next to the family photographs and cherished mementos. I wanted to look at it as I played, and I had a sudden, comforting thought that it would be watching over me. Then I noticed there was a message for me, blinking on the answering machine. *It can't be Hans already!* I pressed playback.

'Sarah, it's Miriam. I hope you're well. Can we meet soon? Call me ... lots to catch up.' The message was very brief, but she sounded friendly, much to my surprise. *She must have forgiven me finally, for the Daniel episode. Well, I'm glad, because she certainly has no cause to be jealous now. I wonder what she's been up to lately. We'll be seeing each other in a couple of weeks at college but I'd like to meet soon. I can tell her about my adventures in Austria!* I called her back and we arranged to meet the following day for lunch, at The

Gatehouse. There was so much to talk about, but we agreed to wait until we met, for a proper chin wag.

The next day dawned clear and breezy. As I strolled to the restaurant, a hint of golden autumn colour in the trees and a nip in the air told me my silver summer was over. It had all been just a summer fling after all, doomed to fizzle out with the approach of cooler weather and a return to the daily grind. My break-up with Hans didn't feel like grief. There was sadness, but it felt more like relief.

Miriam was sitting in the beer garden when I arrived, and she waved me over to her table, which was sheltered from the wind. I hardly recognised her. Her long, mousy brown hair had been cut and styled into a chin-length bob, with blonde highlights, which made her look very modern. She was wearing a red cashmere jumper and black leather trousers. What a transformation!

'Miriam! What have you done to yourself? You look fabulous!'

'Thank you. You look pretty good yourself. I heard through the grapevine you went to Austria on holiday in June, then went back recently. So why did you go back? Something must have happened there. Come on, out with it!' We ordered drinks and I started to tell her about my adventure in Mayrhofen, which was how it all started, but when the drinks arrived, I stopped. Miriam was making a point of waving her left hand in the air as she sipped her drink with her right hand. The diamond in the ring was huge. Its size and brilliance reeked of money, so the topic of conversation immediately changed.

'Miriam, are you engaged?'

'Isn't it obvious? I thought you'd never ask.'

'Who ...?'

'You'll never guess.'

'Do I know him?'

'Oh yes, you know him very well.' One person immediately sprang to mind.

'Daniel?' Her sly grin told me I was right. I was speechless. *She transformed herself and won him back, well no wonder she's so friendly with me again, look at her ... she's gloating.*

'We're getting married next summer, after I finish the teacher training course, and we plan to buy a house in Hampstead, or maybe Highgate, so we'll be neighbours. Wouldn't that be great!' I smiled and nodded as I sipped my wine and tried to imagine Miriam and Daniel as neighbours. The thought had never occurred to me that they would end up together and certainly not living nearby. I knew Daniel's family was rolling in money and he was probably making a mint in his job as a stockbroker. *What a surprise! Miriam has finally hooked herself a big fish.* I wished my own future was so clear, but I congratulated her, and we spent some time discussing her plans for the wedding until she suddenly stopped and leaned forward.

'Sarah, enough about me and Daniel, I'm dying to hear about your holidays in Austria!' There was a delay as the waitress brought menus and we pored over the selections. Miriam found out I was vegetarian as well as kosher, which amused her.

'No more burgers for you then, and certainly not cheeseburgers. You used to inhale them!'

'I guess we all change ... in one way or another.'

'Now, what happened in Austria? Did you meet the love of your life?' She listened as I told her about my accident in Mayrhofen and about being rescued by Hans and Max, interrupting me to ask for more details about them, mainly what they looked like, then letting me continue. I told her about Hans's invitation to visit him in Vienna, the sightseeing, the silver bird, meeting his mother.

'Did you make love? Of course you did! Was it fabulous? Of course it was!' I told her about my initial warm feelings for Hans, about the fun we had, as she nodded enthusiastically. Then, when I told her about the break-up, she frowned and sat back in her chair.

'Are you crazy? Explain!' so I did.

'What about Max? He sounds more your type.'

'He is Miriam! Max is the one for me and he's coming to London in December so ...'

'That's great! Don't let this one get away! Will I get to meet him?'

'I'm not sure.'

'Sarah, are you ok? You've been fumbling with your cutlery, and you seem a bit distracted.'

'If you must know, I've been having a few problems with my hands shaking sometimes, and my eyes getting a bit blurry. My left foot drags a bit too when I walk. Hans noticed and he made me promise to see my doctor for a check-up.'

'I should hope so! Look, it's probably nothing serious, but it's better to make sure.'

'I'll call and make an appointment this afternoon. Now, shall we splurge on dessert?'

Hans called me the next day, to make sure I had made an appointment with the doctor. He was in the workshop, so he could only speak for a few minutes, and he didn't mention the break-up, which made me wonder if he was in denial.

'Please let me know the results of the appointment and take care of yourself.'

'Of course, Hans. Thank you for calling. I'll call you when I get any news.'

The next two weeks were taken up with consultations, first with the GP and then the neurologist, followed by a series of tests and an MRI scan. My symptoms had eased up somewhat, but I was getting increasingly anxious as the days passed and there was still no definite diagnosis. Finally, on the day before my college course was resuming, I received a call from the neurologist to see him that afternoon. It could only be bad news, and it was. From the pattern of my symptoms and the results of the tests and MRI scan, I was showing early signs of Multiple Sclerosis. I felt sick.

'Are you alright? Would you like a glass of water?' I nodded and then sipped the water as I struggled to take in what the doctor was saying.

'It's more than likely the most common, relapsing remitting type. This means that your symptoms will tend to worsen and last for several days or weeks or months, then slowly improve over a similar period. The relapses, often associated with periods of stress or illness, may occur without warning, and the periods between attacks, the remissions, could last for months or years. Every case is different, so it's difficult to be sure how yours will develop. I'm very sorry Sarah.'

'Is there no ... cure?' I stammered, looking up at the doctor, expecting a miracle.

'I'm afraid not. However, there is medication that will help to ease and manage your symptoms when they occur. This must come as quite a shock to you. You'll need some time to come to terms with your illness. I'll give you some information to read and refer you to a counsellor. Also, there are support groups which are available to you. I would urge you to attend, especially as you live alone. You'll see you're not the only one dealing with this.'

It was the sheer unpredictability of it all that hit me the hardest. *How on earth am I going to be able to complete my course and then hold down a teaching job, knowing that my symptoms could return at any time, affecting my eyes and my whole nervous system. I wouldn't even be able to play the piano. Why me and why now? God help me!* I collapsed onto the sofa and broke down in sobs when I got home.

Hans had been calling me regularly for the past few weeks, but I had no news for him until now. The next morning, after a restless night with little sleep, I called him just before I left for college. I didn't want to talk to him for too long. When I gave him the news, he didn't respond right away.

'Hans, are you there?' When he finally spoke, there was a slight catch in his voice.

'Yes darling, I'm here and I'm so sorry. Can I do anything to help?'

'There's nothing you can do Hans, you're so far away, but thank you for caring.'

'Please call me at any time if you need to talk ... and I hope to see you again one day.' There were tears in my eyes as I hung up the phone. He had finally accepted it was over.

In keeping with the neurologist's prediction, my symptoms had improved, so I decided to hope for the best and continue with my course as planned. Miriam caught up with me the next day in college. She gasped when I told her my news, then hugged me.

'Oh Sarah, I'm so sorry! But I'm glad you're going to carry on with the course. Good for you!'

I had to disclose my health problem with the college to continue with my studies, but because my symptoms had eased and I was otherwise fit and healthy, I was allowed to complete the course. The autumn whirlwind of classes, studies and tests proved to be a welcome distraction, as there wasn't much time to wallow in self-pity. Miriam was my study buddy, so bright and bubbly now, she carried me along with her, making sure I kept going. Our friendship had reached a new level. Seeing her with Daniel, who was now more serious and more mature than I remembered, made me realise how much I needed someone in my life too, especially now. I felt so alone, and grief suddenly gripped me again. Tears stung my eyes and I felt like I couldn't breathe.

First my parents, then my horrible diagnosis and Hans is gone now too, and even though I was the one to end it I still miss him sometimes. I must pull myself together. It's for the best ... but some days were a confusing blur, and I had trouble focusing on more than one thing at a time. I kept putting off the counselling and support group sessions, but I knew, from the information the doctor had given me, that my illness could begin affecting my brain. I played the piano most evenings, mainly Mozart sonatas, to work through my grief and confusion, but the silver bird, hovering over me, was a constant reminder of Hans, so I listened to Mozart's Requiem instead.

December arrived with a wintry blast. I received a phone call from Max one rainy morning, which instantly transformed my mood, and my hand shook when I heard his voice. He gave me the details for the matinée concert in London the following week and we made plans to meet afterwards. I decided not to tell him about my illness yet, but I did mention the break-up with Hans. He expressed his condolences, but I sensed he wasn't at all surprised.

9. Max

December ushered in a whirlwind of activity for the orchestra. Preparations for the upcoming tour kept me very busy, but not too busy to contact Sarah, as promised. She sounded very tired when I called, but nonetheless happy to hear from me. I hadn't seen Hans for ages, so I didn't know they had broken up, until she told me. I felt sad for them both, but thinking back, I wasn't surprised.

Hans is kind and generous and he's a talented silversmith with a successful business, so he has a lot to offer her. He's been a good friend to me, but I've noticed whenever I've visited him at home he seems to be under the thumb of his mother. She can be charming, but I know from experience she's intolerant of anyone who doesn't conform to her own beliefs and very strict standards of behaviour. I noticed her raised eyebrows and felt her icy stare when I told her I believe in music and nature and the wonders of science, but I don't believe there's a god in the formal, religious sense. She didn't argue with me or try to convert me, but she was very cool towards me after that, and Hans stopped inviting me to his place. I wonder if Sarah's Jewish faith may be part of the reason for the breakup. She's also honest and outspoken like me, and she was beginning to take up a lot of Hans's time and affection ... so ...

'Sarah, I'm sorry to hear you and Hans have split up. What happened?'

'I don't really want to talk about it now Max, but I think it's for the best.'

'I haven't had a chance to speak to Hans lately, but I'm sure he's gutted!'

'It was difficult for me too, and I've had a difficult time recently for other reasons, but I'll fill you in when I see you. Will you be coming to London with the orchestra soon?' She sounded brighter as we discussed the schedule for my arrival in London and the concerts at the Royal Festival Hall. We planned to meet up the day after I arrived, the day of the first concert. She said she would take the tube into central London and attend the concert, a matinée performance. There was no evening performance that day, so I suggested we go for dinner afterwards.

'That would be lovely Max!' The growing excitement in her voice was matched only by mine.

'Excellent! It's a date then! I'll call you again as soon as I arrive in London. Take care!'

London was heaving with Christmas shoppers, and I had to dodge my way back to the hotel along the glistening pavement, through a forest of waving, weaving, multi-coloured umbrellas. The tinny sounds of carols came at me from everywhere and I cringed, pulling the collar of my overcoat up to try to muffle the noise, but there was no escape. My brief attempt at sightseeing had been aborted by the weather and the solid wall of screeching traffic and scuffling humanity. Settling back into my hotel room, I hung up my drenched overcoat, took a hot shower and then poured myself a stiff drink. Sarah's voice was like soft, soothing music to my ears when I called her. I could visualise those big dark eyes in that beautiful face, the flowing cascade of her hair and the curve of her breasts. What a temptress. I had to contain my impatience to see her as we made plans to meet after the concert the next day. That night I lay in bed, imagining what it would be like to make love to her, after which I drifted off and slept like a log.

The concert was fully booked. As the conductor made his entrance to the podium, I made a furtive attempt to scan the clapping audience, searching for Sarah, but no luck. Knowing she was out there somewhere in the crowd was enough to inspire me and I poured more than my usual heart and soul into my performance. We began with a few seasonal, crowd-pleasing pieces, like Mozart's Musical Sleigh Ride. Following the brief interval, we launched into yet another Mozart crowd-pleaser, Eine Kleine Nachtmusik, finishing up with his more serious March of the Priests, from Die Zauberflote. It seemed more fitting to the seasonal devotions than the raucous Strauss Radetzky Marsch, which we usually finished up with in Vienna. I couldn't wait to get off the stage, but the audience wanted an *encore*, so I contained my impatience as we complied with a lively rendition of the well-worn piece from our repertoire, the Overture to *The Marriage of Figaro*.

Sarah was waiting for me in the foyer. I sensed immediately that something was wrong. She looked lovely, as always, but she was fidgeting with her programme and there was a pallor to her face that I had only seen once before, during her rescue in Mayrhofen. We hugged tightly.

'Sarah, it's lovely to see you again! Let's get out of here. I've booked a table at ---'

'I loved the concert Max, and you were wonderful, but I'm not feeling that great.'

I put my arm around her waist and steered her towards the exit. We had to wait a few minutes in the queue for a taxi, and she leaned heavily against me. I decided against going for dinner.

'I think we should skip dinner Sarah and just get you home. The tube will be crowded, and you're not well, so I'll come with you and see you get home safely.' She nodded, relieved. The taxi driver took us to Waterloo, the nearest tube station, and Sarah explained we would need to take the Northern Line to get to Highgate. It was a long journey and as we sat close together on the tube, she told me about her illness and how the symptoms had returned, which explained her exhaustion. I found it hard to accept that this vibrant young woman was beaten down by an illness which had no cure, which was unpredictable in its attacks, and would be an affliction for the rest of her life. I instinctively put my arm around her and pulled her closer. She sighed and rested her head on my shoulder. My voice was hoarse as I tried to console her. I felt so bloody helpless.

'Darling Sarah, I'm so sorry, and you've been suffering alone. What can I do to help?'

'Thanks, but there's nothing you can do Max. Now, let's talk about something else.'

But I couldn't think of anything worthwhile to say. I glanced down at her. She was still very pale. Her eyes were closed, so I just let her rest quietly against my shoulder as the rowdy, beer-soaked crowd jostled and joked around us. I was suddenly struck by the random cruelty of life. Why should someone so young and lively and intelligent, like Sarah, be targeted? If I wasn't completely sure of my feelings for her before, holding back out of respect for Hans, they crashed in on me now that Hans was out of the picture. *She's so beautiful she takes my breath away ... and my chances with her have changed for the better ... she's so vulnerable right now ... she needs me.*

Sarah was dozing and I was daydreaming, so we almost missed Highgate Station and had to make a mad scramble, clearing the exit just before the doors closed. The taxi driver seemed to know Sarah and chatted away to her, but she just answered politely, not in the mood for gossip. Sarah's townhouse was situated in a lovely area and though it wasn't as large and impressive as some of the neighbouring properties, it looked nonetheless quite charming and attractive.

'Please come in Max and make yourself at home. We've missed dinner, so you must be hungry. Can I get you something to eat?' She started rummaging around in the kitchen.

'No, you need to relax. Let's just order something. Are you ok with pizza?' She laughed.

'Vegetarian pizza's fine. The number for the local pizzeria is next to the phone. I'm going to get changed. I always feel so grubby after that stuffy tube.' I noticed she was limping as she made her way to the staircase and slowly pulled herself upstairs, holding on to the banister. I had to stop myself from rushing to help her. I knew that wouldn't have been a good idea as she was learning to cope with her illness in her own way. I turned away and picked up the phone, ordering two pizzas.

As I waited for her to come back downstairs, I surveyed the living room. My eyes were drawn immediately to the piano and the various objects neatly arranged on top. Right in the centre was a striking silver bird with a gold beak and I suspected it must have been from Hans. There were some candlesticks, maybe for Shabbat or some other Jewish ceremony, and a few photographs, probably of her parents and other relatives. I could see the family resemblance to one dark-eyed, attractive woman, who must have been her mother. There were several other photographs, somewhat faded, hanging on the wall next to the piano. I guessed they must have been older relatives and perhaps some were survivors or victims of the holocaust. She had told me a little about them that last evening in Vienna, when Hans was too drunk to care. The silver bird was so finely detailed, I picked it up to examine it more closely.

'Isn't it beautiful! Hans made that for me, and I'll always treasure it.' I replaced it carefully on top of the piano and turned to face her. She was standing in the entrance to the living room, dressed in a thick, fluffy, white bathrobe, which was a great camouflage, but I had x-ray vision.

'I hope you don't mind, I had to get comfortable.' I just stood there, grinning, as she continued, 'Why don't you remove your bow tie and unbutton your penguin suit a bit – relax!' She smiled and I noticed the colour had crept back into her cheeks and her eyes were bright again. The doorbell rang and I went to answer it, paying for the pizzas and taking them through to the kitchen. We sat at the kitchen table, like an old married couple, munching pizza and sipping red wine. She refused to discuss her illness, so we talked about anything and everything else. Her frequent smiles and laughter told me she was happy, and it made me happy to know that I was the reason.

During our impromptu, casual dinner, I told her about my family background. Not much to tell there: parents divorced and living separate lives in Geneva, and one married sister in Vienna, who has never forgiven me for 'abandoning' and then divorcing Marta, her best friend. Because of this, we hardly ever saw each other. In response to Sarah's questions about Marta, I explained about her inability to accept the demands of my musical career, my frequent touring with the orchestra, and her subsequent drinking bouts, which led to some nasty shouting matches.

'We married too young, Sarah, and it was an unhappy marriage.'

'Do you have any children?'

'No, which is a good thing, because we're not forced to keep in touch anymore.' The rest of our conversation was more light-hearted, and I learned much more about her, like her 'wilder' side, 'fast food and fast boys' - her words - and how she's now mellowed, resulting in her renewed friendship with the 'transformed' Miriam, 'she of the black leather trousers'. She also told me how the Jewish community had been so supportive after the death of her parents. She was enjoying her college studies, determined to finish the course in the summer and hoping she'd be able to obtain a teaching position afterwards. She loved playing the piano and we talked at length about Mozart and her favourite sonatas. I asked her to play something for me, but she declined, saying the wine was making her a bit woozy. I knew I had to make a move, one way or another.

'Well Sarah, you must be tired, and I have to think about getting back to the hotel.'

'Must you? It's lovely to have you here. Why don't you stay, and sleep on the sofa.'

'I suppose I could. Tomorrow's performance isn't until the evening so ...'

'Great! You won't want to face that long tube journey tonight. I'll get you a blanket and a pillow. The sofa is quite comfortable, and we can have breakfast together in the morning.' I couldn't refuse such an invitation. She helped me to get settled on the sofa, kissed me lightly on the cheek, wished me goodnight and made her way slowly back up the stairs. It wasn't exactly how I had wanted the evening to end, but it was enough, for now.

The winter sun, streaming in through the window, told me it was much later than my usual wake up time. Sarah was standing over me, in her fluffy bathrobe, hands on hips, shaking her head.

'It's about time you got up, you old sleepyhead!' She was pretending to sound annoyed, like a school matron. I groaned and swung my legs over the edge of the sofa. The blanket was in a heap on the floor, from my tossing and turning during the night, and my mouth was dry.

'I'll make us some fresh coffee and toast and scramble some eggs while you go and freshen up.' The comforting smell of the coffee, wafting through the house, revived me and I was suddenly feeling ravenous. I returned to the kitchen and stood quietly in the doorway, watching her as she prepared our breakfast. Her face was partly hidden by her morning-tousled hair and her hands trembled a little as she poured the coffee. I was suddenly overcome with such a feeling of love and compassion that it took me by surprise. I wanted to protect her and make love to her. The last thing I wanted to do was leave her. We sat quietly facing each other, drinking coffee and eating scrambled eggs on toast, not talking much, just looking down at our plates and then gazing up at each other, until I could bear it no longer. I pushed my chair back, walked over, gently lifted her hair away from her face, bent down and kissed her. She responded immediately, kissing me back and throwing her arms around my neck as she stood up, pressing her body against me. Her need was unmistakeable, so I loosened her bathrobe and slowly slipped my hands inside, which made her jump, but only for a moment. There was no turning back after that.

We lay closely entwined in her bed that morning, trying to recover from the urgent expression of our pent-up passion. My relief was total and complete from one rising crescendo, but she had several in close succession before she was able to relax. I dozed for a while, then my brain sprang back to life, trying to figure out a way to see her again ... and again ... and again.

'Sarah, I must get back to the hotel and prepare for this evening's performance, but I'd like to come back tomorrow after the final performance, if that's ok. We need to talk seriously before I return to Vienna the next day.' She didn't answer. Her smile told me all I wanted to know.

During the tube journey back, later that morning, my mind was racing along its own track. *Do I really want to get involved again? I've been pretty content on my own for the past few years and I like the freedom. On the other hand, I'm not getting any younger and it would be nice to settle down with someone who needs me and who understands the demands of my career. Sarah and I seem to be well matched, physically and intellectually. Her illness doesn't seem to make any difference, for now, but I'd have to make allowances for her as it progresses and I've always been a selfish sod, or so I've been told. Then there's the practical consideration of where we'd live if we get together. She has a lovely house here and she wouldn't want to move to Vienna, so that would mean me moving to London. Hmmm ... come to think of it there's nothing to keep me in Vienna except my job, and jobs can be changed. There are several great orchestras in London, so I may be able to find a job with one of them. I'll make some enquiries and take it from there.*

The performance that evening left me drained, physically and mentally. I tried to focus all my attention on my playing and set aside the major decisions which were facing me, with limited success. It wasn't my best work. The following day, before the final performance, which was a matinée, I made some telephone calls, trying to assess my chances of finding a suitable vacancy. The resident orchestra at the Royal Festival Hall wasn't looking for a second violinist, so I would need to expand my enquiries to others. The whole process would take time, and as I'd be returning to Vienna the next day, I would have to continue my search from there. This meant I would need to travel back to London, maybe several times, for auditions. This was a prospect which appealed to me, as it meant I would be able to see Sarah again. Meanwhile, I would need to sound her out about us getting together permanently, before considering leaving my current job and accepting a position in London. As soon as the concert was over, I finished packing and checked out of the hotel, declining an invitation from my musician friends to join them for drinks. Carrying my violin case and travel bag, I headed for the tube. The long, boring journey gave me an opportunity to mull over what I would say to Sarah.

10. Sarah

As I waited for Max to return for our 'serious talk', my anticipation was muted somewhat by a niggling worry that my recurring relapses would eventually scare him away. I couldn't deal with any more grief, so I would have to be sure he loved me enough to stay with me through the inevitable ups and downs of my illness. *Pull yourself together Sarah! What if he has no intention of getting together and he's just coming to say goodbye? God! I couldn't bear it!*

As soon as I opened the door and he rushed in, with his violin case and his travel bag and his broad grin, I knew I had nothing to worry about. *He's crazy about me ... maybe he's always been crazy about me ... ever since Mayrhofen ... but Hans was always front and centre with me then.*

'Take off your coat and stay a while Max.' I smiled, like a perfect host, as I closed the door.

'I was hoping to stay the night, if that's ok with you.' He didn't need an answer. He put down his violin case and travel bag, pulled off his overcoat and threw it on a chair. Then he grabbed me, pulling me close, kissing me and caressing me until I playfully pushed him away.

'Let's have a drink first and I've prepared a simple dinner for us this time. I hope you like latkes, which are potato pancakes served with applesauce and sour cream. It's what Mamma always used to make to celebrate Hannukah. I'm trying to keep my family traditions alive. I can cook something different for you if you prefer.'

'No! That sounds delicious and it's great that you keep the traditions alive. It must be quite a challenge to celebrate Hannukah when Christmas celebrations seem to overwhelm everything else at this time of year. Do you light the special row of candles too?'

'The menorah. I wasn't going to do it this year because the memories might be too painful, but now you're here and I'm not alone, at least for this evening, I think I'll light the first one.' I took the menorah from the top of the piano and placed it prominently on the living room windowsill. 'This will announce to anyone outside that Hannukah is being celebrated in this house'. Max watched me as I took a match and lit the shamash, the tall helper candle, and then used it to light the first candle of the menorah. It felt symbolic somehow, of my new beginning.

We sat on the green velvet sofa, in the soft glow of candlelight, sipping our kosher wine.

'How are you feeling now Sarah?'

'Much better. My symptoms have eased, so I think they're in remission.'

'Good! You must keep me informed and let me know if I can help in any way.' Then he plied me with questions about Hannukah and other aspects of my Jewish faith. I couldn't help thinking how he differed from Hans in that regard. Some of his questions were challenging.

'Don't all religions pray for the return of the light in the middle of winter darkness? Even the pagans did that, at the winter solstice, so how is your celebration any different or more religious than the others?' He was forcing me to defend my faith, which no one had done before.

'It's not just the return of the light. I admit this lighting of candles may have been borrowed from the pagans, but the Christians have borrowed it too, with their Christmas tree lights. Maybe it stems from a basic human need for light. However, during Hannukah it recalls a couple of historical events, just as Christmas recalls the birth of Jesus.'

Max smiled and took my hand in his, as I explained first about the successful rebellion of the Jewish people against the persecutions of the Syrians in the Maccabean War, during the second century BCE. The rebellion was led by Mattathias Maccabee and his five sons, who defeated the Syrian forces and rededicated the Jewish Temple in Jerusalem with an eight-day celebration of lights.

'So, it's a celebration of a military victory?'

'Well, yes, but the rabbis were uncomfortable with this, so they preferred another story to justify the eight days of lighting candles and merrymaking. According to the other story, the Maccabees found a single jar of consecrated oil, which was used to keep the Eternal Flame alight in the Temple. There was only enough oil to last for one day, and it would take eight days to get more. Miraculously, the oil lasted for eight days, so instead of the military focus, God's miracle became the central part of Hannukah's message of dedication and the survival of Judaism.'

Following our traditional dinner of potato latkes, which Max ate with lashings of applesauce and sour cream, we cleared the table, and he insisted on helping me with the washing up.

'Sarah, now that's done, let's sit on the sofa. I have something to ask you.' He steered me back to the living room and as we sat there, he kissed me gently, then took my hand.

'How would you feel about us spending more time together ... I mean a lot more time?'

'I'd love that Max, but what do you mean exactly? You live in Vienna.'

'Yes, but that can be changed. I have nothing to keep me there. I'm divorced with no children, and I'm not close to my parents or my sister.'

'What about your job with the orchestra?'

'I've started to make some enquiries about getting a job with one of the orchestras here and I'll continue my search when I get home. It's going to take some time and I'd need to come back here for auditions, maybe several times,' as he squeezed my hand, then continued, 'but before I go any further with this, I need to know that if things work out, I'd be able to move in with you here.'

'You're asking me for a commitment?' I was thrilled but decided to play him along a bit.

'Well yes Sarah, I guess I am.' I hesitated and stared down at the carpet, frowning slightly.

'I'm not sure about this Max. It would be a big step and I'm getting used to living alone.'

'So am I! But surely there are benefits, for both of us, to live together, help each other.'

'Is that the only reason you want to do this?' I was still staring at the carpet.

'No.' His voice was low and slightly hoarse, as he lifted my face up to his and answered.

'I love you. I held back before because of Hans. I thought you two were getting serious.'

'Oh Max! I thought so too, but it was just infatuation, but with you --' I couldn't contain myself any longer, throwing my arms around his neck, murmuring that I loved him too. We stumbled up the stairs, unbuttoning clothes, then fell onto my bed for another passionate, prolonged session of lovemaking. Afterwards, as Max slept, I wondered if my strong feeling for him was love after all or just physical need. *There's no question about his feelings for me. He's willing to switch jobs and leave Vienna for me. My illness doesn't seem to bother him right now and I'm going to need someone strong like him, but he needs to make a firm commitment.*

The following morning, I decided to test the waters before he had to leave for Heathrow.

'Max, last night you asked me for a commitment. I would love for you to move in here, but as you said, it's going to take some time for you to find another job and make the move from Vienna. Commitment works both ways, so how do I know you're serious about all this? I don't want to wait for you, then you change your mind about moving ... or maybe you find someone else.'

'I won't change my mind and there won't be anyone else.'

'But I need to be sure. Are you serious about us, or just wanting to shack up with me?'

'Well ...', but he didn't continue, as if he was weighing up what he would say next.

'You see, you're not really serious!' I shouted angrily and pushed him away. There was a brief, pregnant pause, when neither of us moved or spoke, then ...

'Sarah, I won't get down on my knees, but will you marry me?' My plan worked!

'Oh, of course I'll marry you!' I was breathless as he grabbed me and kissed me.

'Okay, the next time I'm in London we'll go shopping for an engagement ring, how's that?'

'That's the kind of commitment I was hoping for!' We hugged tightly, lingering over another kiss until the taxi arrived. Then he rushed out, leaving me standing there, flushed and smiling.

When I told Miriam what had happened, she couldn't resist applying some friendly pressure.

'That's wonderful! I'm happy for you Sarah, but make sure Max buys you that ring the next time you see him, because until then, you're not properly engaged. I don't want you to be hurt.'

For the next couple of months, I was busy with my college course, and managed to get through the mid-term exams with respectable marks, despite my distraction and excitement about Max. He telephoned regularly and it was lovely to hear his voice, but it was taking longer than we had anticipated for him to secure an audition in London. Finally, he called me one evening in March. He told me he had two auditions booked for the following week and he would take the whole week off. We'd be spending the week together, and I was looking forward to our special shopping trip.

That week with Max flew by much too quickly, carrying me along in such a swirling cloud of romantic bliss, that it almost blotted out the anguish I felt as my symptoms returned. Max was a bit nervous about his auditions, so I tried to conceal my pain and discomfort from him, but it was no use. He kept bringing me breakfast in bed and helping me up and down the stairs. I had to insist that he stop fussing and focus instead on his music for the auditions that week with the London Symphony Orchestra and the Orchestra of the Royal Opera House. I waited with bated breath for him to return from each one, scanning his face as he walked in the door, trying to guess his reaction. I needn't have worried. He was smiling both times, saying he was confident that he'd be hearing some good news soon. His optimism lifted my spirits and eased my pain.

'Now that's over Max, do you think we could go shopping before you return to Vienna?'

'Shopping? Why?' He casually poured himself a drink and settled down in Papa's old chair. The pause confused me, and my tears started to well up, until I saw his sly grin.

'Max! You're just teasing me!'

'Am I?'

'You know what you promised.'

'Come here!'

I hesitated, then limped over to him. He pulled me down onto his lap, caressing my face.

'Sarah darling, I'm a man of my word. Sorry if I upset you. I just like to tease sometimes.'

'So, we can go shopping for a ring tomorrow?' He mumbled an answer as he kissed me.

It wasn't quite as large or as brilliant as Miriam's ring, not on Max's musician salary, but it was more beautiful than hers, in my opinion, with a sparkling solitaire diamond, set in white gold. I wore it proudly. I had to pinch myself that I was going to become

Max's wife and my brain was whirling already with initial plans for the wedding.

'I know we can't set a date yet, not until you accept a job offer, but it would be lovely to get married as soon as you move here, and this summer in the synagogue would be perfect.'

'Hey! One step at a time!' I wouldn't let him finish, and he didn't argue the point after that.

I had never doubted his musical virtuosity, which I had experienced first-hand in Vienna, so I was delighted, but not surprised, when a month later he received a job offer with the Orchestra of the Royal Opera House, Covent Garden. When he called to tell me about the offer, he sounded hesitant.

'I'm not sure if I want to accept it. I need to think it over, look at other options.'

'But if you wait too long, they'll withdraw the offer, and it's a terrific opportunity!'

'I suppose so, but it's a big step and I'm quite comfortable here.' I heard a chuckle.

'Max! Stop teasing me!'

'Sorry! To put your mind at rest, I've accepted the offer, but the job doesn't start until early August, in time to prepare for the autumn and winter ballet and opera season. That gives me time to get things sorted here, as I need to sell my flat. I've given notice at work.'

'That's wonderful!' I almost dropped the phone. 'So how soon will you be able to move?'

'I've already put the flat on the market and hope to be out of here as soon as it's sold.'

'So, we'll be able to have a summer wedding!'

'It looks likely, but let's discuss it when I'm there next week. Keep the bed warm!'

The Schönbrunn Palace Orchestra was leaving on tour, but Max had decided not to go with them. He still had a few days holidays left, and he wanted to use them up before leaving his job at the end of June. Before he arrived for another visit the following week, I met Miriam for lunch. We compared notes, or rather we compared rings and discussed wedding plans, even though I hadn't yet discussed mine with Max.

'Max isn't Jewish, so our wedding will have to be a scaled down version of the full Jewish ceremony, and we'll need the Rabbi to approve, or else it will have to be a civil ceremony.'

'But it would be a shame if you can't get married in the synagogue!'

'Maybe the Rabbi will approve it, since Max has no religious affiliation, and providing we agree to set up a Jewish home and raise any children as Jews, it should be fine.'

'In that case, you'll have to do some sweet talking with Max, so good luck with that!'

'We haven't set a date yet, but I'll tie him down to that when he arrives.'

'Yes, don't let him wriggle out of it, especially if he'll be moving in with you soon.'

'Can you believe we may both be old married women by the end of the summer!'

'Hey, we need to graduate first and find teaching positions. Any luck with that?'

'To tell you the truth Miriam, I haven't done anything about it yet, and anyway ...'

'Are you okay? What's wrong?' She leaned forward, touching my hand, suddenly serious.

'I'm not sure I can cope with a permanent teaching position, with my health problem.'

'So why don't you apply for a part-time job as a teaching assistant and see how it goes?'

'I suppose I could, but I've been thinking about doing something else, something that would give me more flexibility, to ease up a bit, as and when I need to.'

'Like what?'

'Like setting up my own business as a private piano teacher. I've always wanted to do that, and I already have a few potential students lined up. Mamma's old friend, Ruth, knows so many people in our community and she told me there are some parents willing to pay for their little darlings to learn to play the piano or to improve their skills. She mentioned it to me because she knows about my illness, and she wants to help me. So, what do you think?'

'Wow! You're a dark horse! I had no idea, but that sounds perfect. Good for you!'

'I haven't discussed it with Max yet, because I had to think it through, but I'm sure now.'

'I suppose you won't need a steady income if Max has one, and you own the house.'

'I'm not worried about money. I just want to keep busy doing something worthwhile.'

'Sarah, you amaze me. You're coping so well. Max will be proud of you.'

Max arrived with his usual flourish the following week and I told him about my plans. His reaction mirrored Miriam's, so the decision was made, and I could concentrate on passing my final exams. During his short visit, I broached the subject again, of us setting a date for the wedding. I told him I wanted the date to be confirmed before he moved in with me. He accused me of extortion, but I knew it was just his teasing again. We agreed that I'd check possible dates with the Rabbi.

'Are you okay with us getting married in the synagogue? You did say you're not religious.'

'I'm fine with it and no, I'm not religious in a formal way, so I have no preference as to where we tie the knot. I would like to know what to expect though, so I don't look like an idiot.'

'Don't worry, I'll brief you, and we'll need to meet with the Rabbi beforehand anyway, so I'll arrange that. It won't be the full Jewish ceremony, just a few of the key elements. When we meet with the Rabbi, we'll need to promise to set up a Jewish home and raise our children as Jews.'

'What? I'm not sure about that Sarah. I can't promise that. If that's a condition for marrying in your synagogue, maybe we could just get married in a civil ceremony and be done with it!'

'Please Max! My parents were married in the synagogue, and I have my heart set on it.'

'I don't like making promises I can't keep.'

'But you won't have to take that responsibility, because I'm the Jew, so it's up to me.'

'Well ...' he hesitated, so I kissed him and continued quickly, before he could object.

'You don't have to convert to Judaism or be directly involved in anything to do with it. It's much more open and liberal these days, so leave that to me and you can still be a heathen!'

'Please Sarah, don't be crass. I believe in many things, universal things, probably more than you do, like the miracles of nature and the wonders of science and the power of music and ...'

'And love?' He didn't answer, but the smile on his face told me he'd surrendered.

Before Max returned to Vienna, I contacted the Rabbi to discuss our situation, to ask for approval and possible dates for the wedding, preferably in July. To my relief, there were no initial objections from the Rabbi, just a requirement for both of us to meet with him first. As Max was due to leave in a couple of days and the Rabbi had some time available the following day, the meeting took place sooner than we had expected. The Rabbi was satisfied, after questioning Max at length, that he would be a support to me in setting up a Jewish home, following Jewish customs and raising Jewish children. We discussed a few details of the pared-down ceremony and agreed a date in July when the Rabbi would officiate. Max was suitably serious throughout, but I noticed his eyes glazed over a few times.

It wasn't easy to focus on studying, as my brain was so full of other things, but I scraped a pass and could look forward to graduating with a teaching diploma. That was the spark I needed to get busy setting up my business, and I turned to Ruth for help with securing my first students. My symptoms were still in remission, so I forged ahead, making sure the living room was tidy and welcoming. I placed fresh flowers from the garden on a side table and cleared the piano of clutter, except for the silver bird, which remained in its central position on top. I couldn't bear to move it, as it had been sitting there, watching over me, for so long. Then I got busy planning my lessons for the children who would be arriving soon for their one-hour sessions.

At the same time, I had to arrange the wedding details, like examining and re-decorating the *huppah*, the canopy Mamma and Papa had used. Max and I would stand beneath it to "marry each other." I had to decide on my wedding dress too. There wouldn't be any formal invitations, as my only guests would be Ruth and her husband, Ben, who agreed to be the two required witnesses. I didn't want to make a fuss, but I suddenly realised I hadn't spoken to Max about whether to invite his parents and his sister. I made a quick call to find out. As I expected, he didn't think it would be appropriate, since he hadn't been in touch with his parents for so long, and his sister was still angry with him for divorcing Marta. He said he'd bought the wedding ring, then casually mentioned he'd spoken to Hans. I caught my breath, but he didn't elaborate, and I didn't ask for any details of their conversation.

Miriam was busy with her own wedding plans, which would include the full Jewish ceremony, as both she and Daniel were Jews, and it would take place in the same synagogue, before mine and Max's. Since we were invited, it would help Max to make sense of some of the customs and symbols of my Jewish faith, especially related to marriage. He said he'd make a special trip to attend, and he could help me with the final preparations for our own wedding at the same time. I didn't realise it then, but with all the excitement

100

and stress building up, my symptoms suddenly returned, and I
knew I'd be needing his support more than ever.

11. Max

The Palace Orchestra left on tour, without me this time. I had already said goodbye to my fellow musicians, with a few regrets, but not enough to make me change my mind about the move to London. I was looking forward to my new job with the Orchestra of the Royal Opera House and to beginning a new life with Sarah. There was a lot to do before then. I had been dragging my feet about cleaning up the flat and clearing out the pile of useless junk that had accumulated since I moved in after the divorce. The agent, Karla, had already shown the flat to a few potential buyers, but no luck there and she was brutally frank with me.

'Max, you'll never sell the place in this state! I refuse to show it again until you've cleaned it up, so I suggest you put your free time to good use and do a major spring clean.'

I filled several bags destined for charity, with 'stuff' I never needed anyway. I ran a mop over the sticky kitchen floor and scrubbed the grime-encrusted kitchen sink as best I could, with an old sponge. I wiped down the counters with the only clean cloth I could find and chased a couple of spiders out of a hidden corner. They scuttled away to some other hideaway, to be discovered by the next resident. Then I flicked a dilapidated duster over the furniture, which wasn't mine anyway. The bathroom was quite a challenge. It took me a while to get it looking like a human being had used it, rather than a wild animal let loose from the zoo. I muttered as I worked and wondered how Sarah managed to keep her house so neat and tidy, until I remembered she told me she had a cleaning service. Finally, I gave up, collapsed into an armchair and guzzled a couple of cold beers. That's when Karla dropped in, frowning and shaking her head as she looked around, running her hand over surfaces, looking in cupboards and venturing briefly into the bathroom.

'What have you been using to clean? The counters are greasy and the bathroom ... well!'

'Sorry. I guess I'm not very good at cleaning. I'll give it another go.'

'Forget it. I suggest you call a professional cleaning service asap' as she swept out of the flat.

After booking the cleaning service, which I should have done in the first place, I thought I had better let my parents know about my imminent move and my marriage to Sarah, but we hadn't spoken since they moved to Geneva, so I doubted they would come to the wedding.

It was just as I suspected when I telephoned them the following day. Mother answered and as soon as I heard her voice, I felt a brief stab of regret about not making more of an effort to keep in touch with her and Father. After the usual perfunctory "How are you" greetings, I told her my news and waited, as I heard her catch her breath before responding.

'Well Max ... this is a surprise. I can understand about your career move to London. However, after your previous, let's face it, disastrous marriage to Marta and the hostile divorce, why would you rush into another marriage? How long have you known this English woman?'

'Long enough to know I love Sarah and she loves me. Besides, I'm sick of living alone.'

'There you are then, the real reason, nothing to do with love at all. Is she rich perhaps?'

'She has a nice house in London, but that's got nothing to do with it!'

'I suspect it may have something to do with it, but I'm sure you have feelings for this woman. I hope your marriage will be happy and I wish you luck in your career. Here's your father.'

'Max, what's this about moving to a new job in London and getting married again?'

'Father, I know it's the right move for me. I'm ready to move on with my life.'

'Yes, I do believe you are. Mother just needs some time to get used to the idea, but she'll come around. I wish you all the best, son. Keep in touch. I'm not sure whether we'll be able to attend the wedding, but we'll be thinking of you anyway. Have you told your sister?'

'No, but she wouldn't be too pleased. Marta's her best friend, so we're not speaking.'

'I'll let her know about your move to London anyway, and I won't mention the wedding.'

'Thanks Father and thanks for understanding. I promise to keep in touch more often.'

The all-too-brief conversation with my parents made me realise that I'd been slowly drifting apart from my family and friends. My thoughts turned to Hans, with a sudden pang of guilt, even though he and Sarah were obviously finished, so I knew I'd done nothing wrong.

Still, I haven't heard from him for months. I wonder how he's doing and if I should tell him about Sarah and me. I really should tell him ... he needs to know ... but it's going to hurt him even more than he's been hurt already. He'll find out eventually, but it's much better coming from me directly, rather than him finding out by some other means. I'll give him a call and ask if we can meet for coffee. I'll break it to him then ... we're old buddies after all.

The following day I called his workshop and Joseph answered.

'Good morning, Joseph. It's Max, Hans's friend. Is he available?'
A moment of silence.

'Hello, Max. Unfortunately, Hans is very busy working on a rush order, and he doesn't want to be disturbed. Shall I tell him you called?'

'Yes, and perhaps he would return my call when he has some time. Thanks Joseph.'

Two days later I still hadn't heard from Hans, so I decided to wander over to his shop, to see whether he could spare some time for coffee with an old friend. Joseph was serving a customer when I arrived. No sign of Hans. I waited, pretending to browse the silver displays in glass cases, until Joseph was free. He approached me slowly, shaking his head, his voice low.

'Max, I'm so sorry, but Hans has told me to tell you he's not available.'

'Is he there, in his workshop?'

'Yes, but ...'

Ignoring Joseph's protests, I brushed past him and opened the door of the workshop. Hans was stooped over his workbench, suitably armoured in thick goggles, leather apron and gauntlets, blow torch in hand, attacking a shapeless chunk of metal. When I entered, he looked up briefly, then kept on working. I had to shout over the noise of the blow torch.

'Hans! Old buddy! Stop that for a minute!' He turned off the blowtorch but didn't remove the armour. 'I know you're busy, but I just want a quick chat, to explain.'

'There's nothing to chat about and you don't have to explain anything to me.'

'Look, can we go for coffee somewhere? I'm moving to London next week.'

'If it's about you and Sarah ...'

'Hans, I just wanted you to hear it from me first. Sarah and I are getting married.'

'Well congratulations. Thanks for telling me and I hope you'll both be very happy. Don't bother sending me an invitation as I can't leave the workshop. Now if you don't mind ...' He turned the blow torch back on and resumed his work. As I backed away and retreated from the workshop, I felt sorry for him, and sad that our friendship was over, but relieved that I had finally told him.

The cleaning service transformed the flat and Karla sold it within days, much to my surprise. The move went smoothly, as I had been streamlining and didn't have much to take with me. The only possession I really needed, other than my clothes and a few personal items, was my violin.

Sarah greeted me with open arms when I arrived and a long, lingering kiss and rib-splitting hug, like I was finally home from the war. She pulled me over to the sofa and I noticed her limp was more pronounced. We sat together, holding hands, smiling and gazing at each other.

'My friend, Miriam, is getting married to Daniel in July, in the synagogue, and we're invited. Miriam and I joked about having a double wedding, but ours will have to be more low-key.'

'I guess that's because I'm a heathen.' She laughed at that, but then looked sad.

'I wish my parents were still alive. They'd love you anyway, heathen or not.'

'Well, my parents are still alive, but they won't be coming, and neither will my sister.'

'You've discussed it with them?'

'My mother isn't keen on me marrying again so soon and my sister hates me anyway, for divorcing Marta, but I think my father understands and he'll try to smooth things over.'

'I'm sorry about your family but we don't need them at our wedding. Mamma's friend, Ruth, and her husband will witness it, along with the Rabbi. Ruth has helped me a lot since Mamma died and she's helping me to get my business set up, so I already have my first students booked. Now, let's discuss some of the detail for the wedding. I thought maybe ...'

'Do we have to discuss it now? Come here!' and she melted, willingly, into my arms.

Sarah carried me along with her on a wave of domestic bliss for the next few weeks, as we settled into the routine of living together. The weekly cleaning service did a great job, but I tried to help with other chores, like loading the dishwasher, sorting the piles of laundry, cooking the occasional meal, but she insisted on doing most of it herself. I suspected she was trying to prove she could still do it all, but as I watched her struggle, I knew that, despite her brave smiles, her illness was starting to drag her down and she'd soon be needing much more of my help.

July arrived with warm, glorious weather, so we spent a lot of time relaxing in the garden.

'Sarah, you've done a wonderful job here. Just look at all those roses!'

'That bush with the pink roses was planted by Mamma, so I've been nurturing it.'

'Why don't we invite a few of your friends over? I'd like to meet them.'

'I'm thinking of inviting Miriam and Daniel, so you could meet them before their wedding.'

'Great! Let's invite them for drinks and maybe a few snacks, no need to fuss cooking.'

When our guests arrived, one hot afternoon a week later, there were hugs all round. Then Sarah made the introductions, and we ushered them into the garden, where I had moved the little round table into the shade and Sarah had covered it with a white tablecloth. She had prepared "afternoon tea" with tiny triangular sandwiches, filled with a variety of things, like cheese and cucumber for herself and smoked salmon for the rest of us. Sarah had been trying to stick to her vegetarian diet, but I suspected my presence was making it difficult for her to plan our meals. My diet up to now, in Vienna, had consisted of fully loaded pizzas, bratwurst with sauerkraut and whatever else was easy to prepare. Now, I admired the carefully arranged selection of sandwiches and the colourful cupcakes, which Sarah had bought from a local patisserie. The chilled white wine was kosher. It was too hot to drink tea. We began our socialising by drinking toasts to our upcoming weddings, then settled back to enjoy a relaxing afternoon in pleasant company.

As we chatted, updating each other on the recent developments in our lives, I found myself warming up, in more ways than one, to Miriam, who was not only attractive, but clearly very interested in me. She had turned her chair slightly to face me directly, smiling and laughing often and occasionally crossing and uncrossing her bare legs, which were on display in a very short skirt. Daniel, on the other hand, was trying to impress Sarah with his success as a stockbroker, and she seemed more flushed than usual as he talked to her. I suspected it wasn't the heat or the wine.

We rounded off that stimulating afternoon with more hugs, somewhat sweaty by then, and Miriam's perfume, along with the sensation of her soft, rounded body against my damp chest, added pleasantly to my slightly drunken state. After our guests had left, Sarah started to clear off the table, head down, long hair falling around her face, hands shaking uncontrollably.

'Sarah! Just leave that! I'll clean it up later. It was lovely, but you look exhausted.' She turned to face me, her dark eyes flashing, her whole body shaking now, but her voice was steady.

'You and Miriam obviously hit it off. Did you have to make it so obvious?'

'What are you talking about? We were just being sociable. What about you and Daniel?'

'We've known each other for a while, so we were just catching up, not flirting!'

'Look, you're tired, it's hot and I feel a bit woozy from the wine. Can we leave it?'

There was no further discussion that afternoon. Sarah made her way, slowly, up the stairs and into our bedroom, slamming the door behind her. I thought it best to leave her alone for a while, to rest, so I finished clearing off the table and loaded the dishwasher.

Then I slumped into the old leather armchair and dozed, waking only when I heard Sarah running the shower.

I need a shower too. Maybe she's calmed down now. It's worth a try. Her shaking seems to be getting worse, so perhaps her illness is part of the reason she's so upset. It must be affecting her emotionally, as well as physically. I must try to be patient with her, but it's not always easy.

By the time I had hauled myself upstairs, Sarah had finished her shower and was lying on the bed, spreadeagled, hair still damp, wearing only her thin cotton panties. The whirring table fan was doing its best to cool her down. I was breathing hard but decided to leave her alone for a while as I jumped into a cool shower, rubbed myself down, and relieved my sexual tension.

That evening we spoke barely a word to each other, passing on dinner, as we couldn't be bothered to prepare anything. Then Sarah seemed to slowly recover, playing a few bars on the piano, but she had to stop when her hands shook again. Later, she must have forgiven me for my alleged indiscretions, as she rolled over in bed and smothered my body with passion.

The next couple of weeks passed by without too much drama, as Sarah's symptoms were in remission again and she resumed her playing, which seemed to relax her. I took up my violin to practice also, in preparation for my new job with the Orchestra of the Royal Opera House. It would be starting in mid-August, and there would be a very busy Autumn and Winter season to follow. Sarah and I occasionally played a few simple pieces together, and our duet was a pleasant way to strengthen the bond between us. Our wedding date was supposed to be in early August, but the Rabbi was too busy that whole month with various other functions, so it was finally confirmed for the first week of September. It made no difference to me, as it would be a simple ceremony and I would only need to take a day or two out of my work schedule. We had decided against taking a honeymoon and would plan a holiday later, when I'd be able to take more time off. Sarah didn't mind the delay, as it gave her more time to prepare and her eyes were brighter than usual as she discussed some of her plans with me.

'We'll be marrying each other under a huppah, which is the canopy supported by four poles.'

'So where can we get one of those?'

'I still have the one my parents used for their wedding, so we'll use that. The canopy is Papa's old prayer shawl and Mamma embroidered it. It's a bit faded now, but it means a lot to me.'

'Sounds like a great idea! So, what happens at the ceremony? What do I do?'

'We enter the synagogue together, to music, and proceed to the huppah.'

'Can I play my violin as we enter?'

'Don't be silly ... on the other hand ... why not? It's our wedding.'

'I may be too nervous to play but I'll give it a try. How about "The marriage of Figaro"?'

'No! Something more serious and serene.'

'Let's see ... Mozart's Violin Concerto number three. I'll play a part of the Adagio.'

'I can't remember that one. Will you play it now?'

'With pleasure darling! I know it by heart.' I took my violin out of the case, lifted it to my chin, tried to look suitably serious and began playing. She lay back on the sofa and closed her eyes. As I played for my future wife, she looked so beautiful and fragile, I felt a lump in my throat.

The last week of July brought the whole of London's Jewish community together, or so it seemed, for the traditional wedding of Miriam and Daniel. The celebrations lasted for days, before and after the wedding itself, and I was relieved that Sarah and I wouldn't have to endure the same exhausting rituals. We attended a few of the gatherings. Sarah tried to explain the significance of some of the customs and symbols, like the bride and groom circling around each other during the wedding ceremony, to bind them together and protect them from evil spirits. Then there were numerous songs, prayers, poems and recitals, in both Hebrew and English. I drank too much wine and joined in the dancing a few times, but I noticed it was all a bit too much for Sarah. She just sat quietly in a corner, then asked me to take her home early.

'I'm sorry I dragged you away Max. You seemed to be enjoying yourself.'

'It's all a bit much don't you think? I'm glad our wedding will be a simple affair.'

'We'll be just as married as Miriam and Daniel because we'll fulfil the key requirements.'

'What are they?'

'We'll marry each other in front of two witnesses and the Rabbi will recite the prayers to consecrate the marriage. Oh, and the bride must accept a gift from the groom.'

'Will the wedding ring suffice? I've already bought it.'

'Yes of course. You see, all the rest of the rituals are just customs and tradition, which would be expected of us if we were both Jewish, but in our case, we can easily dispense with it. You've already promised the Rabbi that you'll support me in establishing a Jewish home and raising our children in the Jewish faith.'

'Yes, so I have. But surely children tend to choose their own religion, or no religion, once they're old enough to make up their own minds. I'll support you anyway darling.'

'I hope so, because I do want children. My illness won't be a barrier to that.'

'Whoa! Let's wait a bit. It's a big step and parenting is exhausting.' She just smiled, and I realised she could just stop taking the pill, whenever she felt ready for motherhood.

12. Sarah

August finally arrived, after a sweltering, stressful July, stressful for me anyway. My symptoms had been getting worse during the relapses and I couldn't hide them from Max. I was limping so badly sometimes that I was afraid of falling, and the numbness and tingling in my hands and feet kept me awake at night, which only added to my general feeling of fatigue. I worried that Max, who seemed to have boundless energy, would get bored with me. I was feeling irritable too, fed up with the heat and with my illness and sometimes I took it out on Max, but he'd been so loving and patient. To top it all off, I couldn't help feeling envious of Miriam, with her big wedding and her blonde highlights and her figure-hugging, low-cut, silk dress, which showed off her curves. No wonder Max was attracted to her. *Huh! I remember her when she was just mousy Miriam.*

'Sarah! Your student is here. Shall I let her in?' Max was standing at the window. Without waiting for an answer, he opened the door with a flourish and ushered little Rachel over to the piano, chatting with her as he did so. Then he turned to me, frowning slightly, as he left the room.

My students were mainly the young children or grandchildren of Ruth's friends and neighbours, and were mostly beginners, so I was able to teach them and correct their playing without having to play anything complicated myself. However, as the month dragged on, I was becoming more and more convinced that I would never be able to make a go of the business. The unpredictability of my relapses and the increasing severity of my symptoms meant that I had to constantly adapt my teaching approach and even cancel some lessons if things got too much for me.

Max sat me down one day, after a particularly painful session that I had to cut short. He put his arm around me and kissed me gently, but when he spoke, his voice was firm.

'Darling, this must stop! You're a great piano teacher and you've been trying so hard to keep going, but you can't go on torturing yourself like this any longer. I'm worried about you!' I knew he was right, but I pulled away from him, jumped up from the sofa and turned to face him.

'What were my music studies for then, and the teacher training? What was that for?'

'You couldn't know you'd develop this illness or that it would progress so quickly.'

'What am I supposed to do? Just give up? I'm *damned* if I'll be beaten down by this! It's fine for you, you're perfectly healthy and able to play your precious violin any time you feel like it. You'll be starting your new job soon. Well good for you, because we'll need the money. I'm not contributing much and soon it'll be nothing at all. How do you think that makes me feel? I'm useless ... no ... I'm worse than useless ... I'm a bloody burden to you!'

He stood up and stared at me, eyebrows raised, but didn't respond right away. My cheeks felt hot and flushed and tears started to prickle my eyes. I stumbled as I tried to brush him away, but he caught me and held me against him, burying his head in my hair, mumbling in my ear.

'Sarah, my love, I can only imagine how you must feel, but you're not a burden, and you're not useless, you're soon to be my wife. We'll be making a life together here, and we'll face whatever happens together. I need your love and support too. We'll support each other.'

'Max, are you sure you still want to marry me, knowing what you know now?'

'Just try and stop me! But I want you to do something for me. You've been going to your regular doctor's appointments to help manage your physical symptoms, but it may help you to get some counselling as well. I'm sure the doctor will refer you. Promise me?' I just nodded.

Max was soon caught up in his new job and I was left alone for hours on end, usually afternoons and evenings. I missed him terribly and was desperate for company, so I called Miriam and invited her for lunch. She was a busy, married woman now, preparing to start a teaching job, so I wasn't sure if she'd have time, but she sounded pleased to hear from me. She suggested we meet at The Gatehouse, and it would be her treat. The place was packed with professionals, enjoying a pleasant lunch break, but Miriam managed to find us a corner table in the garden. She looked stunning, as usual, not at all the 'school ma'am' type, but her flawless makeup couldn't hide the fact she was looking tired. We ordered drinks and sat quietly for a few moments, leaning back in our chairs, smiling and eyeing each other.

'How are you coping Sarah? I haven't seen you since the wedding and then it was only for a few moments. Max must be living with you now and you must be excited about your own wedding.'

'I'm not coping that well. My symptoms during the relapses are getting worse, but it's not all the time. They're in remission now. I just can't cope with the uncertainty of when the next relapse will come, and I've stopped teaching piano. I just hope I'll be fine for the wedding, although it will be very low key. Nothing like yours! We won't be inviting guests, just Ruth and her husband, as witnesses.'

'Sometimes I wish we hadn't planned such a big wedding. All that fuss! Crazy relatives eating and drinking too much and all those rituals going on for days. And the expense! Still, Daniel's family can afford it so I mustn't complain. I envy you and Max your simple ceremony. I'm so sorry about your illness and all the stress you're under, but it must help having Max here.'

'He's been wonderful, very patient and helpful, but he's started his new job now, so he's not around as much and it gets lonely sometimes. But enough about me! How is married life?' The drinks arrived at that moment and Miriam gulped her glass of wine as if it was water.

'I shouldn't really be drinking this, but dammit I need something!'

'What is it, Miriam? Are you ...?'

'Three months pregnant Sarah and scared stiff. It's freaked out Daniel. We're not ready.'

'Three months! But you must have known before you were married.'

'Stupid me stopped taking the pill ages ago, because Daniel was hesitating about getting married, and I thought I'd give him a nudge. I didn't think I'd get pregnant that soon, but Daniel had to marry me then or his parents would have disowned him. A toast to happy families!' I was stunned, but it explained why she looked so tired.

My own problems were forgotten for the next hour as we picked at our lunch and discussed Miriam's pregnancy. It should have been a happy occasion, calling for congratulations, but Miriam only saw it as a problem, causing friction between her and Daniel. I vowed to myself to be totally open with Max about starting a family. As we parted company outside the restaurant, Miriam grabbed my hand and gave it a squeeze.

'Look Sarah, why don't you and Max come over for dinner one evening next week? You haven't seen the house we've bought in Hampstead. We're not very far away, practically neighbours.'

'Yes, that would be lovely. I'll talk to Max and find out which evenings he'll be free.'

That evening Max came home early as there was no evening performance. I felt better than I had for months, lucky too, compared to Miriam. I hugged him as soon as he walked in the door.

'Hey! What's this?'

'I just feel good, that's all, and I want to let you know how much I love you.'

'That's wonderful Sarah. I love you too and I'm glad we have all evening to --'

'You have a one-track mind. Let's have dinner first. I've been slaving away in the kitchen.'

As we relaxed over our evening meal, Max chatted about his job with the Orchestra and how it felt good to be with fellow musicians again, playing in front of an appreciative audience.

'You must come to one of the performances Sarah. Tosca will be playing soon, so if you feel up to it, why don't you come with me into town one day and we can come home together after the performance. Would you like that?' I had been so bored and hadn't been to town for ages.

'Yes! I'd love to see you in action, and I love Puccini's music. I may fit in some shopping too.'

'That's great. I'll see if I can get you a ticket.' Then I changed the subject and told him about my lunch with Miriam that afternoon, about her pregnancy and her invitation for dinner. I didn't mention the fact she had tricked Daniel into marriage. That would have been disloyal to her and would have added an uncomfortable dimension to the dinner conversation when we met.

'Miriam's pregnant already! Wow, they didn't waste any time. Still, they're married with a nice house and Daniel's rolling in dough, so why hang around, if that's what they want.'

It seemed like a good time to broach the subject of starting a family, but Max was in the mood for something other than continuing our conversation.

Lying wrapped in his arms afterwards as he drifted off to sleep, my mind was still wide awake, brooding about a special baby that would be the obvious answer to my boredom.

The following day dawned bright and clear, without the oppressive heat that had hung around for much of August. I slept late and as I rolled over in bed, feeling for Max, who wasn't there, the comforting aroma of coffee wafting up the stairs told me he was making breakfast. Suddenly remembering this was his day off, I decided that this would be the day I'd tell him.

'Time you got up lazy bones! I've made you some coffee and eggy bread, how's that?' He was shouting up the stairs like a sergeant major, so I scrambled out of bed, still stark naked from last night's exertions, pushed my tangled hair away from my eyes and pulled on my bathrobe.

'That's lovely Max, thank you.' He pulled out a chair for me to sit down, kissed the back of my neck then placed a steaming cup in front of me, followed by a plate with enough eggy bread to feed an army. *He's obviously in a good mood, probably because I'm feeling good now.*

'I'm totally yours all day, so what would you like to do?' I needed the right time and place.

'I'd like to go for a walk as it's such a lovely day. Waterlow Park isn't too far from here and you've never been there. We can walk over after breakfast and enjoy the sunshine.'

'Good idea. I'm feeling a bit flabby from riding the tube to work, then sitting for hours once I get there, so I'm in desperate need of exercise' as he devoured several slices of eggy bread.

The park was exactly as I expected it to be on a sunny day, nearing the end of the school summer holiday. It was resonating with the laughter of children, and as we sat on a bench and watched the youngsters feeding the ducks, several young women walked by, pushing prams.

'Max, I'd like us to talk about starting a family.' No answer, so I continued, 'I'd like it to be soon, because if we wait too long my illness may progress to the point where I'll find it difficult to cope with a child.'

'What brought this on? Is it because Miriam is pregnant?'

'No! This is nothing to do with her. This is about us and specifically my ability to cope, which is fine now, but the longer we wait the more difficult it's going to be. Your job is going well, and the house was paid for long ago, so we can afford it, even though I'm not earning any money.'

'Don't you think we should get married first? After that, we can pull out all the stops!'

He was grinning as he spoke, knowing full well we'd be married in two weeks. I had expected a lengthy debate about the pros and cons of parenthood, so his immediate, positive response took me by surprise, and my heart was so full, I felt as though it would burst.

'Oh Max!' was all I could say, considering the lump in my throat and the tears in my eyes.

'Sarah, it may not happen for a while, not like Miriam, so don't get too worked up.' I nodded, but my mind was already turning the guest bedroom into a nursery, with a rocking chair and a teddy bear and a musical mobile and ... *I'll have to shop for baby clothes as soon as it happens.*

The preparations for our simple wedding paled in comparison with my imagined preparations for motherhood. Not entirely imagined, because I stopped taking the pill right after that sunny day in Waterlow Park. I knew Max suspected, but I also knew he wouldn't mind. *Not like Miriam and Daniel. I'll call her and postpone dinner with them until after our wedding ... too stressful.*

The day of our wedding dawned, and the mid-September weather was kind to us. We rose to a pale pink sunrise painting the few cotton-wool clouds floating on the breeze, and as the sun rose higher above the horizon it highlighted the hints of gold in the tall trees lining the crescent. We shared a simple breakfast of coffee and toast ... no eggy bread that day. I had chosen a plain, knee-length, white linen dress and flat shoes, so I wouldn't worry about losing my balance. Max was dressed in a navy suit and striped tie, looking very handsome, but more like a businessman than a groom. I had no more regrets about not having a big wedding and, for various reasons, I no longer envied Miriam. I was a happy bride, and more relaxed than I'd been in a long while.

'Don't forget your violin! You promised to play some Mozart as we walk in.' He grabbed it.

Ruth and Ben came to collect us in their car. We had been managing up to now with walking, taxis and the tube. Ruth hugged me, smiling broadly, as Ben shook Max's hand.

'How are you feeling Sarah? You look lovely, doesn't she Ben?' He nodded and grinned.

'A bit nervous, but not as much as I thought I'd be, thanks to you two and your support.'

'Yes, thanks!' Max added, helping me into the car for the short trip to the synagogue.

The Rabbi greeted us, and I noticed my parents' huppah was already in place, thanks to Ruth. There was nobody else in the synagogue, just the Rabbi, Ruth and Ben, Max and me and it would have been deathly silent if not for Max and his violin. The processional was slow and stately, in keeping with the Adagio from Mozart's Violin Concerto number 3. I glanced at Max as we walked together, and I noticed his cheeks were flushed as he played. *He's nervous. I've never seen him nervous. This is a big day for him too. Oh ... Mamma and Papa ... I wish you were here.* Max stopped playing as we stood close together under the canopy and the Rabbi addressed us both, with a brief nod to Ruth and Ben.

'Welcome in the name of Adonai.' I was relieved that he spoke in English. Then he recited the prayer asking for God's presence and blessing of the marriage.

'Splendour is upon everything,
Blessing is upon everything
May the One Who is full of this abundance
Bless this groom and bride.'

Then there was a long pause as the Rabbi waited for us to proceed with the core of the ceremony. I nudged Max and for a moment he just stared at me, wondering what came next. Then suddenly remembering, he fished in his pocket for my wedding ring. The Rabbi nodded.

'Repeat after me.' Max did as he was told, but his voice was low and almost inaudible.

'By this ring, you are consecrated to me, in accordance with the traditions and the laws of Moses and Israel.' I then repeated the same words as I received the ring, and we were married!

The Rabbi congratulated us and wished us a long and happy life together. He reminded us of our promise to keep our home in the Jewish traditions and to raise our children in the Jewish faith. Max was fidgeting during that bit. Ruth and Ben hugged us, and we were free to leave the synagogue after the very brief ceremony, just as married as if it had taken days of ritual.

'Time to celebrate! Come back to our place and let's have champagne.' Ruth had put on quite a spread, so we spent the rest of the day eating and relaxing with them and getting slightly drunk. Max played a tiddly overture from The Marriage of Figaro to enthusiastic applause.

We had decided to delay a holiday abroad until the following summer, when Max would be able to take more time off. So, our honeymoon consisted of three days at home, relaxing in the garden in the mild autumn weather, spending long, lazy, mornings in bed, making love in the afternoon too, and playing some piano and violin duets. I couldn't remember ever being so happy before, even during those special days which I spent in Vienna with Hans ... dear Hans. I often wondered how he was doing now and if he'd found someone else ... someone acceptable to his mother. The silver bird was still perched on top of the piano, a comforting presence and a constant reminder of him.

Max returned to a busy autumn schedule at the Royal Opera House, and I made several trips to London, making the most of my relatively stable health situation to browse the shops for baby furniture and baby clothes. Max kept telling me to wait until we knew for sure, but I couldn't stop the growing tide of excitement and anticipation at the possibility of conceiving a child. Then, one blustery morning in October, Miriam called. I felt guilty that Max and I still hadn't accepted the dinner invitation, but when I started to apologise, she stopped me.

'Sarah, that's not why I'm calling. Something's happened and I just need someone to talk to. Would it be alright if I come and see you this afternoon, if you're alone?'

Miriam arrived an hour later, her face pale and streaked with tears, her body trembling as we hugged. I'd never seen her in such a state. I led her to the sofa, and we sat down, close together. I remained silent, waiting, while she just stared at the carpet, before turning to me.

'Oh Sarah! I've had a miscarriage. I've lost the baby!' There was a sudden lump in my throat.

'No, that's so sad Miriam. I'm so sorry.' I took her hand and stroked it gently.

'Daniel and I aren't ready for parenthood, so I think he's relieved, but I ...' she couldn't go on, and I realised her grief was genuine, so I grabbed her and hugged her tightly as she sobbed. I had prepared a light lunch, but she wasn't hungry, and left soon afterwards. Max came home late. I waited up and told him the news. Then I stopped shopping for baby things.

13. Max

I was almost totally immersed, during the autumn and winter, in my role at the Royal Opera House. There were so many performances and rehearsals that season that I was often home very late, and Sarah no longer waited up for me. I did manage to get her a ticket for one of the Tosca matinées and she took the tube home alone afterwards, as I had an evening performance. When I asked her about it the next day, she said only that the opera was quite good, but the long tube ride home was very tiring, and she wouldn't want to do it again, not all by herself.

'Maybe I should have got a ticket for Miriam as well, so she could have gone with you.'

'Yes, well you didn't. Anyway, Miriam doesn't like opera.'

'How do you know that? She might have enjoyed it!'

'Look Max, don't argue with me!'

'I'm not arguing with ---'

'Yes, you are! Do you think I don't know my own friend?'

'Sarah let's just forget it. I'm sorry you've had to spend so much time alone.' I grabbed her hand and pulled her to me, but she pulled away and stumbled into the sofa.

'See! I can't even walk properly!'

'Are you having another relapse?'

'Isn't it obvious? My medication doesn't prevent them, just eases them.'

There were frequent, similar relapse episodes that winter and Sarah was becoming increasingly irritable. I tried to be understanding, considering her struggle to control her tremors and then her bodily functions, but I couldn't help resenting her lashing out at me whenever I tried to help her. She had a medical support team that helped to alleviate her physical pain, but she refused to get counselling for her emotional pain, and I was a poor substitute for a qualified therapist. We did have some calmer episodes during the remissions. We continued trying for a baby, as the doctors told us that it wouldn't affect the course of her illness. She should be able to have a normal pregnancy, with less frequent relapses, and be able to deliver a healthy baby.

When I finally managed to get Sarah pregnant, the cold, wet winter was giving way to a warm, wet spring. Our feelings of relief and joy were muted somewhat by what had happened to Miriam and Daniel, and by the niggling worry of how we'd be able to cope with the constant demands of parenthood. Sarah had morning sickness, but that just seemed to reassure her.

'Darling, it's wonderful, but let's wait a while before you run out and start buying things.'

'I know! Don't keep on at me! Can't we at least start redecorating the guest room?'

I didn't have the heart to refuse her, so I spent a lot of my free time cleaning and painting and silently wondering at my transformation from my selfish, independent, former self, into a caring, supportive husband and father-to-be. As the months went by that spring, she continued to blossom and she was becoming much more dependent on me, not just during her now less frequent relapses, but much of the time.

We visited Miriam and Daniel several times in their large, rambling house in Hampstead. Daniel was obviously doing well in The City and keen to let us know, but he didn't seem that interested in my work. He was an arrogant sod, but I put up with him for Sarah's sake, as she and Miriam seemed to enjoy each other's company more than ever. I couldn't help noticing that Daniel and Miriam showed little affection towards each other, no smiles or hugs, not even touching each other. Sarah hadn't noticed, or at least she never mentioned it and I said nothing. Then Miriam managed to get me alone in the kitchen a couple of times, presumably to ask me privately how Sarah was coping. At least that's how it usually started. However, as we chatted, she'd edge closer to me, lightly touch my arm, then my hand, then smile and fix her steady gaze on me until I found myself transfixed by her bright blue eyes. She wore too much make-up, but she was an attractive, seductive woman and her interest in me was both reassuring and tempting, especially as Sarah was beginning to lose interest in the physical side of our marriage. It was the combination of her pregnancy and her illness that caused her to refuse my repeated advances in bed, so I had to resign myself to quietly relieving myself. My thoughts began to turn more and more to Miriam, and to planning how we might steal some time together.

As the almost incessant April rain gradually gave way to a balmy, brighter May, Sarah became even more dependent and demanding of my time, openly resenting my busy schedule and long hours in London. There was no pleasing her and my feelings of frustration increased.

'Look Sarah, I'm trying to be patient! I understand it's not easy for you, coping with your illness, but you haven't had a relapse for a while and your pregnancy is going well, so surely ...'

'No, you *don't* understand! It's not my illness or my pregnancy! It's *you!* You can't wait to leave in the morning and when you get home it's usually very late. When are we supposed to spend time together?' Her eyes, those beautiful, dark eyes, were beginning to fill with tears.

'But darling, we do spend time together, on my days off. Like yesterday for instance ...'

'Oh sure! A few hours working on your own in the garden, then you spent the rest of the afternoon practicing your violin, and most of the evening you had your nose in a book!'

'So, what was I supposed to do?' Her eyes were suddenly glinting angrily, her voice raised.

'Talk to me! Take me out for a nice meal. Talk to me about this baby ... our baby!'

She had a way of making me feel guilty and I suppose she had a point. I had been focused on my own feelings lately, not catering to her needs as much as I did before. So, I tried to make it up to her for the next few weeks, making time to just sit and talk about the baby, taking her out for lunch several times, taking over most of the household chores and trying to be supportive.

Then something snapped in me. I just wanted to escape from Sarah's incessant demands. The answer came to me when Miriam appeared at the door one day in early June. Perfect timing. Sarah had taken a taxi to an appointment with her doctor, and I was alone.

'Hello Miriam, you've just missed Sarah. She's gone to the doctor, but please come in.' I must have been grinning like an idiot. Miriam, smiling back at me, strolled in, parked herself on the sofa and ran her hand slowly over the velvet seat cushion beside her. She leaned back, still smiling, and crossed her shapely legs. I stared at the carpet and offered to make coffee.

'No coffee for me thanks. Come and sit down and tell me how you're coping these days.'

'Well, I ...' After a moment's hesitation I sat across from her, in the old leather chair.

'It must be a challenge for you lately. I know Sarah's been quite moody, which is to be expected I suppose, but still, it's not easy for you.' I fidgeted and changed the subject.

'How is Daniel?'

'Oh, I hardly ever see him. He's always working on some big deal or other. He's doing well of course, but we're not getting along, if you know what I mean.' She smiled, uncrossing her legs. I knew exactly what she meant. I rose from the chair, walked over and sat down beside her on the sofa. We turned to face each other, our eyes questioning, silently searching, and she was about to speak, when suddenly I pulled her towards me. She pressed her body into mine and kissed my cheek. Then her lips found mine. After a few minutes we pulled away, breathless.

'I'd better go before Sarah gets home,' she giggled and stood up. I just sat there, unable to move or speak. I was roused, racked with guilt, shocked at my behaviour. Miriam rearranged her blouse and skirt. She turned back to face me, her face flushed, eyes shining, voice soft and low.

'You don't have to feel guilty, Max. I don't. Daniel and I aren't making love much anymore. I suspect he's got a lover in town. I know you love Sarah, but you have physical needs that she's probably not able to meet right now. She doesn't need to know about this. I'd like to see more of you, nothing serious, just an occasional get-together.' I still couldn't move or speak, but I didn't need to say a word. She grabbed her bag, walked towards the door then turned.

'Why don't you give me a call when you know you'll have some free time in London, and I'll take the tube down and meet you there.' Her confidence astonished me, but I couldn't resist.

Our affair in a London hotel continued throughout that summer. Our meetings only lasted an hour or two. They were intense, exciting and focused entirely on our physical needs, so it was all we needed. There was no need for conversation, and we parted immediately afterwards. I was still feeling guilty, but I was much more relaxed and supportive with Sarah, who was blooming with our growing baby. My summer workload had eased somewhat, so we spent more time together, shopping for nursery furniture, baby clothes and numerous other accessories that Sarah assured me would be essential. I doubted a tiny baby would need quite so many things, but I went along with it most of the time to humour her.

Miriam still came to visit, but we were careful to stay out of each other's way as much as possible. She seemed relaxed and confident, and Daniel never came with her. Most of the time she and Sarah sat chatting in the garden and I found an excuse to be elsewhere in the house. I'm sure Sarah had no idea about the affair. Anyway, I didn't want to hurt her.

September and October ushered in a flurry of rehearsals for the upcoming autumn and winter season at the Royal Opera House, so my time was starting to get squeezed again. Sarah's health seemed to be more stable now, with very few relapses, and she no longer complained about my long hours in London. She was keeping herself busy preparing for the baby's arrival, due sometime in December. We knew it was a boy, which meant a lot of blue in the nursery.

'I hope he'll arrive in time for Hannukah. That will be a very special celebration.'

'Will our son have to be circumcised? I don't see why a baby should have to suffer that.'

'He won't feel a thing. The doctor will make sure of that and yes, it's important for every Jewish male to be circumcised. It represents the sacred bond with God.'

'Honestly Sarah, I fail to see how removing the foreskin can be a bond with God!' She sighed and continued explaining the ritual to me in detail, how it had been an essential part of being Jewish, through the ages. I just nodded and said no more, just to keep the peace. With Sarah's enthusiasm for fulfilling our promise to the Rabbi, to maintain a Jewish home, I began to wonder if I would have any say at all in our child's upbringing.

One late October evening I arrived home to find Sarah perched awkwardly on the piano stool, hair falling softly around her face, steady hands moving over the keys, oblivious to me or anything else, totally immersed in playing Mozart's Piano Sonata No. 12. I stood watching her, with a sudden lump in my throat, and I was glad my affair with Miriam was over. During a leisurely breakfast the next morning, Sarah asked about my parents.

'Max, why don't you call them and tell them about the baby? I know you haven't been in touch for ages, and you don't get along, but they need to know they'll be grandparents.'

'Yes, I guess I should. I'll call them later today.'

'Invite them over for Hannukah, or Christmas, or whenever the baby's born.'

'I doubt they'll come but I'll invite them. I know my sister Ingrid won't come.'

'I wish Mamma and Papa were still alive. They'd be over the moon about the baby!'

To my surprise, Mother was delighted to hear the news, so her previous reluctance to accept my marriage to Sarah, so soon after my divorce, was no longer an issue. She promised to come and visit as soon as the baby was born. Father was pleased to hear he'd soon be a 'grandpa', and to my relief, he said he'd let Ingrid know. I suspected that my relationship with her was beyond repair. Sarah was happy to hear we'd be having family visitors to help us celebrate the birth.

'They never came to our wedding, so I've never met them, and it's about time.'

'I agree. Hopefully, we can all get along.'

'Why shouldn't we? Our baby needs a family connection. He'll draw us all together.'

'Darling, of course you're right!' Her self-assurance dispelled any doubts I might have had.

'We need to choose a Jewish name for the baby. I'd like us to name him Jacob, after Papa.'

'That's a good name ... fine by me.'

Jacob was obviously impatient to be born, because Sarah went into labour prematurely in late November and we ended up spending agonising hours in the maternity ward, worrying

128

if he would be strong enough to survive. The nurses assured us everything looked normal for a safe delivery, even though he was three weeks early. I tried to stay calm and positive for Sarah as she bravely endured the labour pains, totally exhausted. But I was terrified. Nothing in my life up to that point had prepared me for the birth of my son. The medical staff made sure all the necessary preparations were in place for a premature birth, giving Sarah special injections, which would help the baby's lungs to breathe properly, and preparing an incubator. They seemed confident that he would be fine, with some extra special care.

After an eternity, Sarah was wheeled into the delivery room, with me following closely behind. Nothing would keep me out, and they encouraged me to be present. I was suitably gowned and stationed where I'd be able to hold Sarah's hand and provide encouragement. As the moment of birth approached, she was squeezing my hand so hard the pain became almost as unbearable as hers, but not quite. Then they administered an injection into her spine to ease the pain. She had, thankfully, decided against a completely natural birth. One final push and ...

'Sarah darling, I can see his head! It's turning slowly ... and now I can see his face!'

'Who does he look like?' The rest of Jacob's body slid out and he was whisked away.

'I'll tell you when he's been cleaned up.' My eyes followed the tiny bundle, which was quickly wrapped in a towel and carried to another part of the room, to be worked on by the nurses.

'Why isn't he crying? I can't hear him crying!' No sooner had she spoken than we heard what sounded like a little squeak, and then a soft, pitiful little cry that tugged at my heartstrings.

Sarah sank back into the pillow from exhaustion and relief, and I kissed her gently. I was overwhelmed with relief too, and with pride for my wife and new-born son. The beaming nurses brought Jacob back to us. He was red, wrinkly, tiny and fragile and they handed him to Sarah.

'You can hold him, but only for a minute. He weighs just five pounds, so he needs to go into the incubator for a while, until he's a bit stronger, but you can visit him every day. We'll give you both instructions for caring for him once you take him home.' As Sarah cradled Jacob to her breast and kissed the top of his tiny, downy head, I was breathless with a mixture of pride, joy, and terror.

Sarah stayed in hospital for several days, to regain some of her depleted strength. This allowed her to bond with Jacob by stroking him gently through the holes in the incubator, while speaking to him softly. I visited her and Jacob every day. Each time I did my protective instinct kicked in, but at the same time I wondered what would be expected of me as a first-time father. I realised I didn't have a clue, but I was determined to learn. Jacob's helpless, skinny little body felt warm as I tentatively touched him through the incubator holes and watched over him as he slept, which was most of the time. Sarah was learning how to feed him, becoming an expert at using the breast pump. He was being closely monitored in the Neonatal Intensive Care Unit, and as each day went by, my fear for his survival began to subside. I visited the NICU as often as I could, but I returned to work two days after the birth, as it was a very busy festive season.

When Sarah returned home, Jacob had to remain in the NICU for several weeks, so she took taxis to visit him. Somehow, during those first hectic weeks, in between rehearsals and seasonal performances, I managed to get home as often as I could to take care of Sarah, who was beginning to show signs of relapse again, struggling to get up the stairs and dropping things. I was concerned that, without the constant care she had received in hospital for both her and Jacob, she would struggle to cope when we were finally allowed to bring him home. The community nurse would visit for a while, but Sarah needed much more help, and I wouldn't be home frequently enough to provide the level of support she'd need.

'Darling, why don't we arrange to get you some help for a while until ---'

'I'm perfectly capable of looking after Jacob myself!' She glared at me, eyes flashing.

'Yes, I know you are. I meant to help you with the cooking and cleaning.'

'No! I don't want anyone coming in here, fussing and spreading germs around Jacob.'

'Well, let's wait and see how you feel once Jacob is home. We can discuss it then.'

Sarah's fierce refusal of help worried me. I waited until she was asleep and then I called Ruth. She had provided Sarah with lots of practical help in the past.

14. Sarah

Jacob was still being cared for in the NICU two weeks after I gave birth. I was getting anxious and impatient to bring him home, because my daily trips to the hospital to deliver my expressed breast milk and provide him with some motherly skin contact were wearing me out. Jacob was having some problem with his lungs, which weren't yet fully developed. He was on oxygen and couldn't be moved from the incubator as he also needed some help regulating his temperature. Max was very supportive, but after a week he had to return to work, leaving me to cope alone. Hannukah was approaching, but I couldn't care less as there wouldn't be much of a celebration. One drizzly afternoon, as I lay on the sofa worrying about Jacob, the doorbell rang.

'Ruth! Come in, but I'm afraid I'm not very good company right now.'

'My dear, you must be feeling overwhelmed. Max told me about Jacob. Congratulations!'

'Thank you, but I can't bring him home yet. I'm having to traipse back and forth every day.'

'At least he's well cared for and I'm sure you'll soon have him home. Can I help with anything?'

'Like what? I'm the only one who can feed him and there's nothing to do here.'

Ruth was glancing around the room, probably checking for dust and general clutter. There was plenty of that ... as if I had the time or energy to do any cleaning ... and Max was no help now he was back at work. Ruth sat down next to me on the sofa and took my hand.

'Sarah, I know you're worried about Jacob, but the best thing you can do for him, except feed him of course, is to take care of yourself. You need to build up your strength while you have this time to yourself to recover. Once he's home you won't be getting much sleep for a while.'

'I know! So, what am I supposed to do? I don't think I'll be able to cope, and my illness makes it ten times worse! You're very kind Ruth, but I wish Mamma was still here!' My eyes were welling up and my hands started to tremble, so I pushed Ruth's hand away and struggled to get up. Then I sat back down again as I felt dizzy and faint, just as everything went black.

When I came to, I could hear Ruth on the phone talking to Max, and I was being carried out to the waiting ambulance. They told me I was suffering from general fatigue and dehydration and would need complete rest. I was to remain in the hospital overnight and they wouldn't even let me visit Jacob. Max arrived at the hospital very late, just as I was drifting off to sleep, jolting me wide awake.

'Sarah, get up! We need to get to the NICU now! Jacob is struggling!'

Sitting bolt upright on the edge of the bed I almost fainted again, but a nurse arrived with a wheelchair. She helped us to negotiate the endless maze of hallways as we raced to the unit.

We both knew, as soon as we entered, before we even saw Jacob, that something was seriously wrong. The doctor came slowly towards us, hands outstretched, starting to mumble something, but Max pushed him aside and rushed to the incubator. Ignoring the doctor, I pulled myself out of the wheelchair and limped over to join Max, who was bending over Jacob, so tiny and fragile and so perfectly still in his incubator. The doctor stood next to us.

'He's gone. I'm so sorry. We did what we could, but he was suffering from a combination of factors and ...' Max turned suddenly to face the doctor, eyes wide, face red, voice raised.

'What factors? Don't talk to us about factors! He was improving, doing well, until today!'

What followed was a long, medical explanation of the cause of Jacob's death, something to do with his lung capacity, plus a heart murmur and some bleeding on the brain. Jacob had "put up a brave fight" but in the end, even with care and medical help, it had all proved too much for him. As we stood there, I froze. I was unable to move or speak or feel anything. Max did my moving and speaking and feeling for me, shouting at the medical team, grabbing me in his arms and hugging me, then sobbing silently into my neck. My body felt numb. Then the pain began. I sank back into the wheelchair, my arms and legs twitching with painful tremors. I couldn't even cry out. I just sat there, watching Max as he carefully lifted Jacob from the incubator and held him close to his chest. He turned to me, his face composed now, his voice soft and low.

'Nothing can hurt him now. Do you want to hold him?' I shook my head.

'No, I'm too shaky. I might drop him.' Max bent down and held Jacob against my heart.

The next few days were spent in a medicated haze, as my painful relapse was worse than ever, and I knew there would be no remission for the pain in my heart. Somehow Max and I got through it all, but I finally broke down and cried aloud, during Jacob's brief funeral in the synagogue, when the Rabbi began to recite the traditional prayer over Jacob's tiny, plain wooden coffin:

'God who is full of compassion, dwelling on high
Grant perfect peace to the soul of Jacob.
May he rest under the wings of your presence
Holy and pure, who shines bright as the sky.'

We were a small group of mourners. Max had informed his parents, who were devastated, but they had decided not to attend. Ruth and Ben were there, along with Miriam and Daniel and a few other members of the Jewish community, some of whom I'd never spoken to before. I knew that the community support was meant to provide comfort, but there was no comfort to be had, from any source, on that day. We made the short trip to the cemetery during a sudden downpour of rain and buried Jacob in a quiet corner. More prayers were recited at the graveside, but I was focused only on the small, dark, damp hole in the ground, beginning to fill with rainwater, as Jacob's coffin was lowered into it. Max was the first to lift a shovel of the muddy earth and throw it onto the coffin, the loud thud making me jump. He tried to hand the shovel to me, but I refused it. I couldn't face the cruel finality of the grave. Throwing wet mud over a baby's coffin made no sense to me. I knew it was a tradition meant to help with accepting the death and beginning the grief process, but I vowed to myself, then and there, that I would no longer pretend to follow tradition unless it made sense and made me feel better. I couldn't accept never seeing Jacob again, never providing him with milk, never gently stroking his warm body as he lay silently in his incubator, his tiny, temporary world. This was the child I had borne for just over eight months and delivered safely, only to lose him so soon afterwards. I wanted to lift his coffin out of that wet, muddy hole, open it up and kiss him back to life, but instead I just closed my eyes and turned away, as the final prayers were said, and the final shovel of mud was thrown.

Returning to the house brought fresh agony, as I stood at the open doorway of Jacob's nursery. His empty cot, his brand-new, smiling teddy bear and brightly coloured mobile were crying out for a child to give them purpose. Then there was the rocking chair in the corner, a safe, cosy place to feed him and lull him to sleep. I hesitated for a moment, then stepped into the room and sat down in the rocking chair. That's where Max found me a few minutes later.

'Sarah darling ...' then he stopped, because he knew there was nothing more to say. He lifted me out of the chair and helped me back down the stairs, depositing me at the kitchen table and ordering me to drink the tea he'd made. There would be no *shiva*. I saw no point in any of the old Jewish traditions for mourners. There would be no sitting on or near the floor, no lighting the seven-day candle, no covering the mirrors. I would mourn Jacob in my own way, in my own time.

Max was much calmer now, compared to his angry outburst and emotional breakdown in the hospital, but maybe he was just being strong for me. He had arranged to take a few days of compassionate leave from work, but we hardly spoke to each other during that time. Ruth came with meals she had prepared, and she offered to stay with me after Max went back to work. I thanked her, but said I preferred to be alone. She understood, but then suggested a grief counselling service that she could arrange for me. I told her I just needed time.

It took several more days before the paralysis inside me started to shift and change until it finally became a churning, burning anger that I couldn't control. Max bore the brunt of it and tried to console me with hugs and kisses, but I just pushed him away. Eventually he gave up trying and retreated into his own grieving process, which seemed so different from mine. One day, when the painful tremors in my body had eased a bit, I sat down at the piano. I hadn't played for so long and as I sat there, running my hands over the keys, trying to decide what to play, I glanced up at the silver bird perched on top. It was bathed in a shaft of pale winter sunlight that had found its way through the living room window. The silver bird's gleaming presence was at once a comfort, and at the same time a reminder of another love, another time, another loss.

Weeks went by, but I was lost in my own painful, solitary world and was only vaguely aware of the days of the week, or the time of day, or the people around me. Max and I weren't communicating, beyond a few passing remarks, as he was spending more time at work and often home very late. Ruth still came every few days to chat, but I didn't feel like talking, so she ended up just tidying up and making tea or a light meal, making sure I ate something. She had arranged for someone from the health service to come, but they weren't much help, so I sent them away. I wasn't sleeping and felt tired all the time. My medication wasn't helping with the pain inside, and one day I played with the idea of ending it all, which scared me and jolted me, for a while, out of my dark despair.

'Hello Sarah, how are you feeling now?' It was Miriam on the phone.

'Oh, you know, a little better, but I ...'

'Why don't I drop by, and we can walk over to the Gatehouse for lunch. It's not too cold today and the fresh air will do you good.'

'But I must look frightful.'

'Nonsense! No-one will care. I'll be there in about an hour.'

A quick glance in the full-length mirror in the bedroom shocked me. I didn't recognise the pale, bedraggled woman with the sad eyes and the wild-woman hair staring back at me. I stood there for several minutes, not sure if this was a good idea, then slowly took off my dressing gown, which I had lived in for weeks and which needed a wash. I stepped into the shower and ran warm soapy water over my hair and body, then rinsed off and dried myself quickly, keeping an eye on the time. The hairdryer was going full blast as I tried to decide what to wear, realising that such a seemingly simple decision now required a huge effort of concentration. As soon as I had pulled on my grey wool trousers and black cashmere jumper the doorbell rang. It rang again, but Miriam would have to wait, while I slapped on some blusher and lipstick and ran a comb through my hair. I limped down the stairs, holding on to the banister, and pulled on my winter coat, hat and gloves.

'You look fine, let's go!' She took my arm to steady me as we walked slowly through the brisk winter air to the restaurant. I noticed it had snowed recently, but the paths were clear. We sat in the restaurant garden, next to one of the outdoor heaters, and ordered a light lunch.

'How is Max? He must be feeling rough, like you. I hardly ever see him these days.'

'Well neither do I. He's in the middle of a very busy season at the ROH and gets home from London very late most nights, then sleeps in until noon. We're finding it difficult to talk, so I don't really know how he's feeling, except that he doesn't seem to feel it as badly as me.'

'You don't know that! He's just coping with his grief in a different way from you, like maybe staying longer than necessary at work and sleeping longer than necessary when he's home.'

'I think he's just avoiding me, and I don't really blame him. I've been a bitch to him lately.'

'Have you? How?' She was starting to pry, and it touched a nerve.

'Oh, I don't want to talk about it.'

'Have you talked to each other about Jacob and shared your feelings about losing him?'

'Not really, but I know we must, sooner or later. Now please let's change the subject. Tell me how it's going between you and Daniel.' She hesitated for a moment, then smiled brightly.

'Much better! My miscarriage was very distressing, as you know, but nothing like what you've just been through. Anyway, after that we had to talk seriously about whether we wanted children and it turns out we do, both of us, just not for another year or two. At least we know where we stand. I think he's forgiven me for tricking him into marriage a bit sooner than we'd planned!'

I sat back and looked at her more closely. She was avoiding looking at me, fiddling with the diamond in her ring. I knew somehow that she was lying. She and Daniel must still be having problems. Well, that was none of my business, so I leaned forward, speaking quietly, honestly.

'I don't think I could face having another child. I couldn't go through this again. I'd always be frightened of it happening again, and anyway my illness would be that much worse.'

'Do you think Max wants another baby?' I sat back again, frowning, and refused to answer. The waiter brought our food, so we had an excuse to stop talking for several minutes. We ate slowly, looking around at the other diners, at the greenery, anywhere but at each other. The awkward silence was finally broken by the return of the waiter, asking if everything was alright. He was referring to the food. We both nodded, and he left, but my stomach was churning. I pushed the remains of my lunch to the side of my plate, put down my fork and faced Miriam.

'Why do you keep asking about Max? You seem more interested in him than me!' She didn't answer immediately, but her face looked flushed as she took two more mouthfuls of food.

'Answer me, Miriam!' My voice was raised, causing our fellow diners to stare. I didn't care.

'Sarah, I'm sorry. I just think you've been so wrapped up in yourself lately, your own grief, that you've been forgetting that Max is going through it too. He's devastated.'

'How do you know how he's feeling? You said you haven't seen him for ages!'

'Well, to be honest I happened to bump into him the other day.'

'Bumped into him! When? Where?' But Miriam didn't answer, and I knew she didn't want to tell me, that she'd already said too much. Something inside me snapped. I rose from the table, stumbling as I did so, dropping my bag on the ground. The waiter rushed to help me.

'Please call me a taxi. I'll pay for my lunch at the till. Goodbye Miriam!' I didn't look back, but I could imagine her sitting there, wide-eyed, staring at me. Maybe I had always suspected her.

When Max returned home that evening, late as usual, I was sitting up in bed, waiting for him. He looked very pale, and his clothes were a bit dishevelled. I'd never seen him like that before and I realised Miriam was probably right, that I hadn't noticed what he was going through. However, I was determined to find out what was going on between them. As soon as he got into bed, before I could question him, he was reaching for me, wanting me, pulling me towards him. I could smell whisky on his breath, which surprised and sickened me, so I tried to resist, but it had been so long, he became insistent and then rough, and I felt too weak and powerless to stop him. Afterwards he just rolled over, exhausted and ready to sleep. As I lay there, sore and bruised, my shock at his behaviour and my suspicions about him and Miriam, gave way to a seething, burning anger. I decided to wait until morning, after he'd sobered up, to confront him.

15. Max

The weeks following Jacob's death were sheer hell, as I tried to make sense of what had happened and more importantly, why it had happened. I knew that premature babies were at risk for certain life-threatening conditions, but the NICU seemed to be experienced at treating them and Jacob was starting to show a few small signs of improvement. Then he suddenly succumbed, and we lost him, just as I was getting used to being a father, just when my instinct to protect him had taken over and I was proud of my son's brave fight for survival. When he gave up the fight, I didn't want to believe it. Within minutes, the anger and bitterness surged up in me. I railed at the doctor and the rest of the medical team, although by then I knew that Jacob's tiny body had developed too many complications and they had done their best for him.

Sarah seemed to be alternating between denial and depression for weeks. Her grief didn't follow the same path or timing as mine. Her illness had flared up, brought on by the stress, so she was in physical pain as well. Eventually her repressed anger and frustration welled up and she started to find fault with me, blaming me for not supporting her more, for not carrying more of the load at home, for coming home late, and on and on until ...

'Sarah, for God's sake, can't you see I'm hurting too?' She turned away, her voice quieter.

'Maybe you are, and maybe losing Jacob was a sign that we're not meant to be together.'

'How can you say that? How can you make that connection? It doesn't make sense!'

'All I know is, I feel like our love may have died when Jacob died.'

She turned back to face me and waited. But I was too tired to respond or argue with her any more or try to convince her of my love. I was beginning to think she was right. She took my silence as my response and made her way slowly upstairs, closing the bedroom door. I was hoping that our shared loss would bring us closer together. Instead, it was driving us apart. The frequent arguments and criticism were wearing me down, so I was glad to be able to focus on work and was in no hurry to get home.

I started to frequent the bars in Covent Garden, sometimes with fellow musicians but often alone, before taking the long tube ride home. One evening, Miriam called me at work, just after a performance. She was in London and wondered if I'd like to meet for a drink. I hesitated, not wanting to get involved again, but I needed to talk to someone. We met in one of the bars. She seemed to understand my grief. She encouraged me to talk about Jacob, listening and nodding as I expressed my feelings of loss to her, in a way that I couldn't with Sarah. Then she asked how we were both coping at home.

'She's struggling Miriam. I'm trying to hold things together and that's all I care to say.'

'I gave her a call today and took her for lunch, got her out of the house, got her to talk.'

'That's kind of you, thanks. Thanks for listening and ...' I stopped as she took my hand, stroking it gently. She continued to stroke it for several minutes, neither of us speaking, which aroused feelings in me that had been denied for too long. I took a deep breath, then took my hand away and grabbed my drink. I asked her about Daniel. She sat back against the bench, crossing her legs, smiling and slowly sipping her drink until she finally answered my question.

'Well, let's just say Daniel and I are trying to hold things together too, but for how long?' We finished our drinks and left the bar. Miriam took my arm as we strolled along, neither of us in a hurry to get home, and we stopped outside the hotel we'd used before. She looked at me, her eyes bright, questioning, hopeful. I thought of Sarah, waiting at home, in pain and grieving.

'Look Miriam, I can't do this anymore. I want to, believe me, but I can't!'

'That's ok Max, I understand. Just let me know when you need me, because you will!'

She sounded so sure of herself, but I wasn't sure about anything, and my head was starting to spin from too much whisky. We took the tube together, not speaking. I dozed most of the way. We took separate taxis home from the station, and I found Sarah sitting up in bed, waiting for me.

'Sarah, I'm sorry. I'm late ... again. You didn't have to ...' but she just stared at me, stone faced. I knew I sounded slightly drunk, and she wanted an explanation, but I also knew that whatever I said would just set her off. So, I said nothing as I undressed, fumbling with my shirt buttons and with the buckle on my belt. Then, leaving my clothes in an untidy heap on the floor, I escaped into the bathroom and splashed some cold water over my face. It didn't help. When I came out, she was lying back against the pillow, looking more beautiful than ever, with her hair soft and tousled around her angel face and her dark eyes fixed on me ... waiting ... and it had been much too long since we had ... and suddenly I just couldn't stop myself.

I'm not proud of what happened that night, my desire for her totally overwhelming her feeble attempts to resist, my falling asleep afterwards, not realising until the following morning what it had done to her, physically and emotionally. When I finally dragged myself downstairs, my head aching, my throat dry, not wanting to admit what had happened, Sarah was sitting at the kitchen table, quietly drinking tea. As I approached her, racked with guilt, needing to apologise, she put down her cup, back straight, eyes closed, flinching as I touched her. I sat down beside her.

'Sarah darling, I ...'

'Get out!'

'What?'

'I want you to leave my house.'

'Look, I'm sorry about last night. I was drunk and I know I must have hurt you.'

'Yes, you did. I've had enough of your selfish, uncaring attitude towards me, cheating on me with Miriam, who's supposed to be my friend. Do you think I'm so stupid I don't know what you've been up to?' I had no answer, just my silence, which just confirmed her suspicions.

'This is my house and I want you out.'

'But Sarah we're married. This is my house too!'

'Not anymore. I want a divorce, but we'll have to start with a separation. You can stay until the end of the week, while you look for somewhere to stay, but you'll have to sleep on the sofa.' I was speechless, and she said nothing more, as she slowly got up from the table and limped over to the sink, rinsed her cup under the tap, took a slice of bread out of the bread bin and popped it into the toaster. Her back was turned, and the silence in the kitchen was palpable until the toaster, suddenly breaking the silence, was almost a relief.

'I'm so sorry, but if that's what you want, I'll move out.' She nodded, her body rigid, in pain.

I should have seen it coming. We'd been avoiding each other for weeks, something I had to admit was mostly my fault, but when we did manage to talk it was usually one-sided, with me listening to her voicing her frustration with her illness, and with the pain and limitations it imposed on her. Then she'd blame me for not being home more often. She never acknowledged my own pain, especially after we lost Jacob. She couldn't even talk about Jacob or express her grief to me, but then, I couldn't talk about it either, except with Miriam, who just happened to be there when I needed her. Sarah had lost all interest in sex, which I know was just another consequence of her illness, but she wouldn't even let me touch her or hold her. Her recent, more frequent relapses had taken a huge toll on her, physically and emotionally, and Jacob's death was the final agony, which tipped both of us, and our relationship, over the edge.

I was living out of my suitcase in an apartment hotel in central London, and in the process of looking for somewhere more permanent there to rent, without much luck. I decided I'd better give my parents a call to explain my current situation. I'd been putting it off as they'd been devastated to hear about the death of their grandchild, and now this ... but Mother was calm.

'Darling, I'm sorry to hear you've separated, but I'm not surprised, after all the stress you've been through. It sounds like Sarah needs a lot of care now, more than you can provide.'

'I know that, but I still love her.'

'Yes, but if neither of you is happy then maybe this is for the best.'

'I'm hoping to find a permanent place to live, but work is taking so much of my time.'

'Why not return to Vienna? You might even get your old job back. You enjoyed it there and you need to get on with your life. Jacob is gone, so there's nothing to keep you in London anymore.'

Following the conversation with them both, I realised how much I missed Vienna and my musician colleagues at the Orangery. Maybe I was just running away, but I decided to take some time off work at the ROH and fly back to Vienna for a short break. Then I'd decide what to do.

As soon as my plane touched down, it felt like coming home. I knew I belonged in Vienna, the beautiful city where I grew up, studied music, made friends ... lost a friend. Settling into the hotel, I tried to shake off the niggling feeling of guilt I still had about Hans, telling myself I'd done nothing wrong, because he and Sarah had broken up before I pursued her and proposed. But I couldn't help wondering how he was doing. We'd been great buddies before … Sarah.

'Hello? Is that Joseph? It's Max, Hans's friend.' Silence, a cough, then a familiar voice.

'Hello, Max. Joseph doesn't work here anymore. This is Hans.' I took a deep breath.

'Hans! How are you? It's been a while. I'm back in Vienna and was wondering if we could meet up for lunch one day, just to catch up.' As he didn't respond, I continued, 'By the way, Sarah and I have separated, a mutual decision. We've both been through hell for the past few months, and I'm moving back to Vienna, hoping to get my old job back.'

'I'm sorry to hear that.' I didn't know if he meant he was sorry about me and Sarah, or sorry I was moving back to Vienna. This wouldn't be easy, but I persisted.

'Look, I thought perhaps we might at least meet up, just once, for old times' sake?'

'I'm busy and short-staffed, so I can't leave here. Well, maybe I could close for an hour.'

We sat across the table from each other in a café near St. Stephens, just as we'd done so many times before. Only this time we eyed each other like strangers, eyes narrowed, voices low. We sat back in our chairs, drank melange and provided each other with an update on our lives since we last met. He told me his mother had suffered another stroke, a major one, and died several months back, so he was now living alone. His silversmith business wasn't doing as well as before, but he was managing okay. As I explained about Sarah, about the progress of her illness, and then about Jacob's death, Hans leaned forward, his voice suddenly hoarse.

'I'm so sorry. You and Sarah have been through hell, but how is she coping alone?'

'Sarah has made it clear she doesn't want me there, and I can't do anything about that, so she'll probably get help from her friends and neighbours in the local Jewish community.'

'I'd like to call her to offer my condolences, if that's ok. Can I have her telephone number?' I hesitated, thinking how the tables had turned. Failing to come up with a good reason to refuse my old friend, I gave it to him. Then we parted company, I suspected for the last time.

When I returned to the hotel, there was a message from my sister, which surprised me as we hadn't spoken since my divorce from Marta. She'd heard that Sarah and I had split up and she suggested we meet for lunch the next day, adding that I might like to know that Marta had stopped drinking and had been asking about me. As I mulled over the lunch invitation, not sure if I was ready for my sister's meddling in my life, I wondered if there was a performance in the Orangery that evening. I called to inquire and, as luck would have it, there was, and there were still tickets available. I couldn't resist the chance to revisit my former workplace, perhaps chat afterwards with my musician friends and hopefully get my former job back. I felt the old excitement returning, as I bent down and lifted my violin out of its case.

Epilogue. Sarah

The winter rain is still lashing against the window and the fire has finally gone out. This old leather chair, which Papa loved, is so warm and comfortable and all-enveloping, it reminds me of his bear hugs, and I don't want to get up. I can feel his presence in the room. Mamma's here too, wanting to know about everything that's happened to me and why I've been neglecting the garden lately. God, I wish I could tell her! God ... what kind of God are you to take everything from me and leave me with nothing? You've taken Papa and Mamma and you've even taken Jacob. What kind of God are you? You've taken my health and left me in pain and disabled and old before my time. Max is gone now too, and I thought Hans loved me, but I guess it wasn't meant to be. I can't even play the piano anymore, it's just gathering dust. If only ... oh, what's the point anyway? Why bother getting up at all? But I'm getting stiff. I've been sitting here too long. I'd better try to get myself to bed ... the phone's ringing ... I must get up now. I struggle over to the phone, on the table by the window.

'Hello?' A familiar voice, that makes me catch my breath.

'Sarah? It's Hans. How are you? Max told me what's happened. I'm so sorry.'

'Hans!' I can't say anything else, as I try to gather my confused thoughts together.

'Look, I don't want to disturb you. I just want to let you know I'm thinking about you and to say how terribly sorry I am about what's happened – the death of your baby – the separation - the progress of your illness – it's more than anyone should have to bear, especially alone.' He pauses, but my eyes are suddenly welling up and I still can't speak, so he continues, 'Sarah, do you have anyone there you can talk to? Is there any help close at hand? I wish I wasn't so far away ...' Then he stops, waiting for me to say something, but his kind words are unleashing a torrent of emotion in me that I can no longer control. The tears are streaming down my face and I can't stifle the sobs that he must be able to hear. He doesn't say anything, just waits, as I continue to sob, trying to release the grief that still overwhelms me. We both know there's no need for words. The silent bond between us speaks volumes and I now realise it's never really gone away. I glance down at the silver bird, still clutched in my hand, and its solid presence comforts me, as always. I finally manage to stop sobbing.

'Oh Hans ... it's so wonderful to hear your voice and so kind of you to call. I'm still struggling to come to terms with everything that's happened ... but I have lots of support here. My neighbours in the Jewish community are making sure I get lots of help at home and Mamma's friend Ruth is making sure I eat properly. I guess I've been neglecting myself lately. I don't need anything really ... at least on the practical side ... but ...'

'But it's not enough, is it? You're having to cope with so much loss and grief. I think I might have some idea of how you're feeling, because I'm grieving too.' I start to wonder why he's grieving too, then he continues, 'Mother died a few months ago from a major stroke, so you see ...'

'Oh! I'm very sorry!' And then a brief pang of guilt, as I can't help feeling relieved that Hans is finally free of her control, and then wondering if this might change anything.

'Thank you Sarah. It's been a bad winter for me too, not just with Mother's death, which was so sudden, so unexpected, but also with the downturn in my business and having to let Joseph go. He's been so loyal and helped me so much. It wasn't an easy decision, but I couldn't afford to pay him anymore. I'm alone in the shop now, so I've stopped accepting orders for new silver pieces as I don't have the time. I need to focus on the customers coming into the shop. I'm just a salesman now.'

'Oh, Hans! That's so sad. You're such a talented artist and silversmith. So, what will happen to your business?'

'I'm thinking of selling it. I already have a couple of interested buyers. It's been my life, almost my entire life up to now, but it's also prevented me from doing other things with my life. I've always wanted to travel, to see a bit more of the world ... the world beyond Vienna!' He laughs, then adds, 'I regret ...' He doesn't continue, but I know what he means. I place the silver bird carefully on the table, and glance out of the window. The rain has stopped.

'Hans, maybe you could start with London?'

❧

BV - #0031 - 201124 - C0 - 203/133/9 - PB - 9781915972552 - Matt Lamination